Readers love
ANDREW GREY

Bad to Be Good

"This book had it all, amazing characters, suspense and an absolutely adorable little boy."

—Paranormal Romance Guild

"Gray has a plethora of passages that convey the essence of his characters and the storyline."

—Love Bytes

Catch of a Lifetime

"…a salute to Mr. Grey's mastery of gay locution, which added enormously to my reading pleasure."

—Rainbow Book Reviews

Paint by Number

"This story, like most of Andrew's books is sweet and full of feelings... If you've never read a book from Andrew Grey and even if you have, I highly recommend this one."

—Open Skye Book Reviews

By Andrew Grey

Accompanied by a Waltz
All for You
Between Loathing and Love
Borrowed Heart
Buried Passions
Catch of a Lifetime
Chasing the Dream
Crossing Divides
Dominant Chord
Dutch Treat
Eastern Cowboy
Hard Road Back
Half a Cowboy
Heartward
In Search of a Story
New Tricks
Noble Intentions
North to the Future
One Good Deed
On Shaky Ground
Paint By Number
The Playmaker
Pulling Strings
Rebound
Reunited
Running to You
Saving Faithless Creek
Shared Revelations
Survive and Conquer
Three Fates
To Have, Hold, and Let Go
Turning the Page
Twice Baked
Unfamiliar Waters
Whipped Cream

ART
Legal Artistry • Artistic Appeal
Artistic Pursuits • Legal Tender

BAD TO BE GOOD
Bad to Be Good
Bad to Be Worthy

BOTTLED UP
The Best Revenge
Bottled Up • Uncorked
An Unexpected Vintage

BRONCO'S BOYS
Inside Out • Upside Down
Backward • Round and Round
Over and Back
Above and Beyond

THE BULLRIDERS
A Wild Ride • A Daring Ride
A Courageous Ride

BY FIRE
Redemption by Fire
Strengthened by Fire
Burnished by Fire
Heat Under Fire

CARLISLE COPS
Fire and Water
Fire and Ice • Fire and Rain
Fire and Snow
Fire and Hail • Fire and Fog

CARLISLE DEPUTIES
Fire and Flint • Fire and Granite
Fire and Agate • Fire and Obsidian
Fire and Onyx • Fire and Diamond

CHEMISTRY
Organic Chemistry
Biochemistry
Electrochemistry
Chemistry Anthology

DREAMSPUN DESIRES
The Lone Rancher
Poppy's Secret
The Best Worst Honeymoon Ever

EYES OF LOVE
Eyes Only for Me
Eyes Only for You

FOREVER YOURS
Can't Live Without You
Never Let You Go

Published by Dreamspinner Press
www.dreamspinnerpress.com

By Andrew Grey (cont.)

GOOD FIGHT
The Good Fight • The Fight Within
The Fight for Identity
Takoda and Horse

HEARTS ENTWINED
Heart Unseen • Heart Unheard
Heart Untouched • Heart Unbroken

HOLIDAY STORIES
Copping a Sweetest Day Feel
Cruise for Christmas
A Lion in Tails
Mariah the Christmas Moose
A Present in Swaddling Clothes
Simple Gifts
Snowbound in Nowhere
Stardust • Sweet Anticipation

LAS VEGAS ESCORTS
The Price • The Gift

LOVE MEANS…
Love Means… No Shame
Love Means… Courage
Love Means… No Boundaries
Love Means… Freedom
Love Means … No Fear
Love Means… Healing
Love Means… Family
Love Means… Renewal
Love Means… No Limits
Love Means… Patience
Love Means… Endurance

LOVE'S CHARTER
Setting the Hook • Ebb and Flow

PLANTING DREAMS
Planting His Dream
Growing His Dream

REKINDLED FLAME
Rekindled Flame
Cleansing Flame
Smoldering Flame

SENSES
Love Comes Silently
Love Comes in Darkness
Love Comes Home
Love Comes Around
Love Comes Unheard
Love Comes to Light

SEVEN DAYS
Seven Days
Unconditional Love

STORIES FROM THE RANGE
A Shared Range
A Troubled Range
An Unsettled Range
A Foreign Range
An Isolated Range
A Volatile Range • A Chaotic Range

STRANDED
Stranded • Taken

TALES FROM KANSAS
Dumped in Oz • Stuck in Oz
Trapped in Oz

TALES FROM ST. GILES
Taming the Beast
Redeeming the Stepbrother

TASTE OF LOVE
A Taste of Love • A Serving of Love
A Helping of Love • A Slice of Love

WITHOUT BORDERS
A Heart Without Borders
A Spirit Without Borders

WORK OUT
Spot Me • Pump Me Up
Core Training
Crunch Time • Positive Resistance
Personal Training
Cardio Conditioning
Work Me Out Anthology

Published by Dreamspinner Press
www.dreamspinnerpress.com

BAD TO BE WORTHY

ANDREW GREY

Published by
DREAMSPINNER PRESS

5032 Capital Circle SW, Suite 2, PMB# 279,
Tallahassee, FL 32305-7886 USA
www.dreamspinnerpress.com

Mass Market Paperback ISBN: 978-1-64108-232-7
Trade Paperback ISBN: 978-1-64405-708-7
Digital ISBN: 978-1-64405-562-5
Mass Market Paperback published June 2021
First Edition
v. 1.0

Printed in the United States of America
∞
This paper meets the requirements of
ANSI/NISO Z39.48-1992 (Permanence of Paper).

To Dominic for all his support,
and to Christi who inspired it all.

Chapter 1

THE MAN now known as Gerome Meadows prowled the beach near his apartment. The sun was so low, its rays just skimmed off the water, turning the tips of the waves red. Gerome wished he could say that this was his favorite part of the day, but he didn't have one. Not here, away from home. Okay, he liked the weather here for the most part. It was February, and back in Detroit they were snowed in under a raging blizzard. But on Longboat Key, Florida, he was strolling the beach in jeans and a light sweatshirt at sundown. This place did have its advantages, but it wasn't home and would probably never feel like home.

The sun dipped farther, now over half gone, the light of the day fading fast. Gerome didn't really care.

He knew how to get back to his place, and no one was going to mess with him. Not if they didn't want to get their nose or legs broken. He was perfectly safe. Hell, on this beach right now, he was the top predator, the one everyone had to watch out for, the caged lion ready to lash out at anything and anyone. Unease crawled under his skin, and he wanted it to go away. Gerome wished he could just accept that his life had changed so much in the past year, but accepting meant giving up the fight. One that, if he really thought about it, he had already lost anyway.

Gerome paused in his stomping gait to watch the sun sink lower behind the water. He bent down and grabbed some shells, which he threw with all his might as though he were trying to hit the damned thing and kill it, send it away. Not that the sun had done anything to him—he just had to try to let go of this unending frustration that hung on like a houseguest who refused to fucking leave. Shell after shell in rapid succession ended up in the water, and nothing changed. Nothing was going to. He turned around to walk back the way he'd come, returning to the life he couldn't escape.

At the path off the beach, with the last of the sun's rays gone, he paused, turning to look out at the blackness of the ocean. A small set of lights bobbed on the water, out far enough that the light itself was all he saw. But as he watched, they came in closer. Another set appeared, exiting the channel to the inner bay, drawing nearer to the other until they met straight out from where Gerome was standing. He crouched, watching and doing his best to blend in with the undulating sand. He could hear nothing over the rolling waves, but the two boats remained near each other for a good ten minutes.

A shout just reached his ears, followed by another, and then they were gone. The boats stayed together for a few minutes after that before separating and going in opposite directions, the first one speeding off into the darkness, the second returning to the bay. Gerome knew he had just seen some sort of rendezvous, and he could only imagine the type of deal that had gone down.

Gerome sat on the sand, the breeze having died to almost nothing, the tiny waves lapping the shore. He closed his eyes.

"Is someone there?" a young voice asked from off to the side.

Gerome didn't move. He just wanted to be left alone. He continued watching, with just enough light to illuminate the figure of a man tentatively approaching the water. The moon must have been rising, providing he could see the outlines of the world around him. "Hello," the guy said again nervously, and then turned back toward the water, continuing his path north along the beach.

The guy was someone to watch as Gerome contemplated his fucking boring, workaday, miserable life—a life that made him want to scream. Back in Detroit, he had been someone important, someone with power and authority. Now he was nothing, the manager of a gift shop. He was once the creative mind behind some of the best gay nightclubs in Detroit. He'd helped build an unwanted part of Detroit's lucrative vice market into a thriving business, until Garvic Senior died and his idiot son took over and decided Gerome and his brothers had to go.

Gerome seethed for the millionth time, knowing he had to let it go and get on with his life. But fuck, what he really wanted was what he once had, and there was no way he was ever going to have that again.

The guy drew closer again, and Gerome could see him more clearly now. He came nearer, checking the shore as he moved. That drew Gerome's curiosity. He waited until the man passed, heading south, and then slowly got to his feet, ambling out to the water's edge. Whatever this guy was looking for, it wasn't likely he was going to find it, not at night. The water gave up her secrets reluctantly, just like Gerome, and she only did it when she wanted to. Still, Gerome wandered the way the guy had come for a little while. He didn't have anywhere he needed to be, and it wasn't late, just dark. He turned back after a while, watching for the other guy but not seeing him.

Gerome figured it was time to go home and let this guy have whatever he was looking for. At the path back to the road, Gerome was about to turn when something tumbling in the surf caught his eye. He checked both ways, but the beach was deserted. He bent down and lifted a floating bundle out of the water. It was wrapped tightly in plastic, and he groaned as he looked it over.

His first instinct was that it was drugs, a bundle packaged for transport, but it wasn't heavy enough for that. Gerome took off his sweatshirt, wrapped the package inside it, and strolled off the beach, across the main road, and down the small side street toward the low apartment building where he lived. Terrance had an apartment there too. Together with Richard, they were as close as—maybe closer than—brothers. Richard was just a mile or so up the road from Gerome and Terrance's building. Thank God the only family he'd ever really had was here with him.

"You want a beer?" Terrance asked from his doorway, and Gerome went right inside and sat down. "What's that?" he added as he handed Gerome the beer.

Gerome set the bundle on the counter and closed the door. "I found it on the beach. I thought I might have seen some sort of transaction offshore, and then a guy wandered up and down the sand. He was looking for something… this, I suspect." Gerome took a swig of his beer as Terrance picked up the package.

"What the hell?" Terrence asked. "This is a bundle of trouble."

Gerome nodded his agreement, but he wasn't too concerned. No one had seen him. "Don't get your panties in a wad." He took the bundle. "I'm not sure what's in here, though."

Terrence got a knife and gently peeled back some of the covering.

"It looks like money," Terrance pronounced. "I'd guess about a hundred thousand, if the bills are twenties. If they're hundreds, about half a million." He lifted his gaze and put the plastic back the way he found it. "What the hell did you stumble on, and what are we going to do with it?"

"I have no idea. I assume it's something that fell into the water during the exchange and it washed to shore. The other man was looking for it, and I found it first." Not that there was a single thing he and Terrance could do about it. They couldn't spend it or put it in a bank—it would draw too much attention to them. He could keep it, but holding a hot potato like this was a risk that could draw even more attention. "I need to talk to Richard."

Terrance sat up. "Fuck, why? He isn't the only one who can think."

Gerome shook his head. "Because he's the one who can help figure out what to do and not screw it up so we end up back in a place like fucking Iowa. Remember?" He growled at Terrance, who puffed out his chest. "I don't like it here, but I *hated* it there, and I'm sure if we fuck it up, we'd be separated."

At one time Gerome, Terrance, and Richard had run the gay mafia business in Detroit. That is until the old man died and his asshole son took over. Garvic Junior decided he was going to take them out, being too squeamish for the "gay" money. They got word and took him down instead by working with the authorities. Now all three of them were in witness protection. Their first stop had been Iowa.

"We all agreed to break the rules in Iowa so we could say goodbye to Mom," Terrance said. "So don't fucking blame me for it."

"I'm not. But getting your ego in a twist because I think Richard could help isn't doing any good either." God, he needed to fucking punch something or someone. Either that or he needed to get laid, bad.

"Fine. Tell him about it when you see him if you want." Terrance drained his beer and picked up another one. "He's working tonight anyway." Terrance was about to open the beer when Gerome grabbed it. "What?"

"Come on. We're going to get something to eat and talk to him. Sitting around here isn't doing either of us any good, and if you drink all that beer, you'll be sick and maudlin as hell." When had their lives become this boring?

"Fine," Terrance grumped and got to his feet. "Let's go." He was already heading for the door. "Where are you going to hide that?" He pointed to the bundle.

Gerome picked it up and took it over to his apartment. He put it in a couple of bags and stashed it in the bedroom behind some boxes in his closet. It should be safe enough there until they figured shit out. He locked the apartment door behind him, and then they got in the car, with Gerome driving, and headed to the restaurant and bar where Richard worked.

"Oh hell," Terrance groaned as they got out of the car. "It's Wednesday."

Gerome smiled and shook his head as they went inside. Coby, Richard's partner's son, hurried out of a booth and right up to Terrance as soon as they walked inside. "I'm having fishies," he told him and waited to be lifted into the huge man's arms. Coby pretty much had Terrance wrapped around his little finger. Hell, Gerome loved the little guy too. Sometimes it was hard to understand or believe just how much their friend's life had changed in the past year.

Richard was the most settled of all of them. He had a husband now, and they were raising Coby together. Gerome would never have thought that any of the three of them would settle down like that, but the proof of how wrong he could be was right in front of him.

"This is a surprise," Richard said as he came over from behind the bar. He paused, looking at both of them for a second before turning away. "Coby, why don't you finish your dinner? I brought you some Sprite."

Coby climbed back into his seat across from Daniel, who watched both of them warily. "What's up?"

"We have a little situation," Terrance said, and Gerome rolled his eyes. "We need to talk."

Richard nodded. "I'll stop by your place when I get off shift." Richard sat next to Daniel for a break.

"Come on and join us," Daniel offered, and Gerome and Terrance slid into the booth. Coby made sure he sat next to Terrance, which Gerome always thought was so cute. Coby was four now, almost five, and he wasn't the least bit intimidated by the fact that Terrance was six three and built like a linebacker.

"Want some fishies?" Coby asked and gave Terrance a piece. Coby was adorable, and Richard looked at Daniel as though he were the center of the world. It would have been enough to make Gerome sick if it wasn't for the fact that he was so jealous, he could spit quarters. Not that he'd tell either of them that.

"I have to go back to work," Richard said a little while later as he squeezed Daniel before slipping out of the booth. "You be good for Daddy, and I'll see you in the morning." Richard leaned over Gerome to give Coby a kiss on the forehead before heading off to the other side of the restaurant, taking his place behind the bar.

"Mr. Gerome, why are you grumpy?" Coby asked before shoving a french fry into his mouth.

"I'm not." Gerome made an effort to smile.

Terrance snorted. "You've been as prickly as a cactus for months." He motioned Andi over. She was her usual bubbly self and took their orders before hurrying away. Gerome noticed that she didn't stick around, though she spent plenty of time talking to everyone else.

"Just admit it, you're grumpy," Terrance pressed. "Own your grump. That's what I say."

Gerome leaned over Coby. "And I say, go…." His anger built, and a steady stream of obscenities flashed through his head. But he couldn't say any of them in front of Coby, which only made him angrier. "Oh hell."

He stood and stomped out of the bar into the parking area, fists clenched.

Fuck it all, he needed to beat the shit out of someone. That would make him feel better and more like a man. All this past year, it had felt like someone had cut his balls off and he was too afraid to do shit about anything.

"Is this the Driftwood?" a vaguely familiar voice asked as a man approached. He was about five eight, maybe, and a hundred twenty pounds soaking wet. It took Gerome about thirty seconds to realize this was the guy from the beach. He recognized the voice.

"Yeah." He decided to play it cool and see if he could get any information out of the guy. He didn't seem too old and certainly wasn't the type to be looking for illicit cash on the beach. There was no smoothness about him, and damn it all, there wasn't a hint of larceny. And Gerome sure as hell knew what that smelled like. What he saw in the guy's eyes was plenty of desperation. "You meeting someone?"

The guy shrugged. "Some guy asked me to try to find something on the beach and I couldn't." He walked to the door, pausing with his hand on it. "Just wanted to tell him."

"It's a big beach out there. Hard to find anything on it most of the time," Gerome observed.

"That's what I told the guy who asked me to look. But he said he'd pay me if I found it, and I could use the money." He went inside, and Gerome followed him, returning to the table, where his food was waiting. He slid back into the booth, not meeting Daniel's gaze. He ate his burger and followed the guy out of the corner of his eye to one of the more remote tables.

"What's with you?" Terrance asked quietly. Coby had climbed into Terrance's lap and was coloring the placemat, having eaten most of his food.

Daniel glared at him. "Are you drunk or something?"

Gerome sighed. "No. I'm fine." He continued watching the dark-haired beauty as Andi approached and then left. The guy had great eyes and was kind of cute, in a lost-puppy sort of way. Dammit, Gerome needed to get his head out of the clouds and off of guys with cute dark eyes, full lips, and some of the most threadbare clothes he had ever seen. Gerome took a bite of his burger, chewing as Andi brought a glass of water and spoke to the guy for a few seconds before leaving the table.

"Daddy, I gotta go," Coby said.

Daniel slid out of the booth and took Coby to the bathroom.

"Okay, what gives? What's with the guy you can't stop watching?" Terrance asked once they were out of earshot.

Daniel was aware of who they were. Richard had told him the year before after they had helped Daniel out of some trouble that wasn't his fault. Hell, if they weren't careful, they were going to turn into fucking Robin Hoods.

"That's the guy who was combing the beach. I think he was looking for the package I found," Gerome explained. "I'm trying to figure out what's going on with him."

Terrance smacked his shoulder. "The kid's a mule, nothing more. Look at him. If he had money coming in, his clothes wouldn't look like they'd fall right off him." He chuckled. "Is that what you'd like to have happen?"

The laughter grew deep and guttural. "Don't look at me that way. I know your type, and that guy pushes all the right buttons." He shook his head. "Come on. This isn't the time for you to get all gooey-eyed over some kid who isn't smart enough to figure out when he's being used." Terrance leaned closer. "Let it go."

At that moment, Gerome wanted to beat the shit out of Terrance, but that wasn't going to solve anything. "Just back off."

A man came inside and went right to the guy from the beach's table. He yanked out a chair, turned it, and sat in it backwards. What a lame move to try to display power. The first guy talked briefly and shrugged, motioning a few times with his hands, probably trying to explain that he had been all up and down the beach. Gerome made note of the newcomer's husky build and too-long dirty-blond hair. But what he noticed most were the expensive slacks, Gucci shoes, and light silk shirt. This was someone who was used to money.

"I won't back off. You have been jealous and snappy for months. I've wanted to beat the living shit out of you at least once a week. What the hell is wrong with you?" Terrance sighed.

"I hate it here. Okay?" he answered. "Nothing ever happens, and all I do is run this little-old-lady gift shop, smile, and act like nothing is wrong. It's boring." He lowered his voice. "The only interesting thing that's happened is the stuff with Daniel and his father, and…." He shook his head. "We were the damned good guys. I hate that. Even today, a brick of money washed up on the shore and we can't do shit with it. Not that it matters. We've got bank accounts stuffed with money we can't access because then the feds will know about them, and if we do anything, Garvic and his goons will figure out where we are—so we're fucking stuck in the most boring place on earth." He shifted his gaze as the guy in the expensive clothes reached for the other man.

Gerome knew a threat when he saw one. The threatening posture was enough to clue him in, let alone the guy's tone. He stood and headed over to the other table, seeing Daniel and Coby leaving the bathroom to return to their table.

"I told you I'd pay you to find that package," the guy hissed just loud enough for Gerome to hear. "You should have kept looking." That tone was very familiar. Gerome had used it to get what he wanted on more than one occasion.

"Did you find what you needed?" Gerome asked as he drew closer, trying to sound like he was asking an innocuous question.

"This is a private conversation," the well-dressed man said with a glare as the guy from the beach paled, looking like he wanted to disappear into the floor. "I suggest you leave!"

Andi put a plate with a grilled cheese on the table in front of Beach Guy and left.

"I'll get out of your hair." Gerome took a step back and turned to Richard, who Andi was speaking with, catching his eye as well before returning to the table.

"Do you think you could get rid of the guy over there?" Gerome asked Terrance. "He's threatening a customer, and I think he needs to leave."

"I'm not on duty," Terrance told him with a wry expression.

It seemed that Terrance wasn't needed. Richard approached the table.

"We're talking," the man in the expensive clothes snapped.

Richard stood his ground. "You're leaving. Threats aren't good for business," he said, pointing toward the door.

Gerome turned away, smiling into his beer as he finished his meal.

"Do you want to know what Cute Puppy Eyes is doing?" Terrance asked.

"Where's the puppy?" Coby asked. "Can we get one?" He bounced up and down, and Gerome mouthed that he was sorry to Daniel. It seemed that getting a dog was his latest obsession.

"Not yet," Daniel answered with surprising patience. "And Mr. Puppy Eyes over there is eating his grilled cheese as though it is gourmet and each bite is to be relished. He also looks really relieved that the guy is gone."

"He's a mule," Terrance repeated.

"What's a mule?" Coby asked.

"Well… they're when a horse and a donkey have a baby," Daniel explained.

Coby stood on the seat, turning in the booth. "He doesn't look like a horsey. He's a man." He turned to Terrance. "You're silly." He giggled as he sat back down to color.

"I think I should take Coby home," Daniel said and began gathering everything up. "It's getting late, and he's going to need to start getting ready for bed. Say goodbye to Mr. Gerome and Mr. Terrance, and then we can go."

Coby of course hugged Terrance and then climbed onto Gerome's lap for a hug.

"Bye." He smiled and then climbed down and took Daniel's hand. After they said goodbye to Richard, they left the restaurant, and Gerome slid to the other side of the table. Andi brought them each another beer because she knew them pretty well, and Gerome watched the object of his attention.

"What's he doing now?" Terrance asked, suppressing a grin that Gerome wished he could smack away.

"You know, someday you're going to find someone who captures your attention for more than just a quick fuck, and when you do, I'm going to tease the hell out of you and make your life totally miserable." Gerome hit Terrance with his coldest stare, only to receive an eye roll in return.

"You can dream," Terrance said. "One thing is for sure: the guy hasn't been eating very much." He drank from his beer.

Andi returned to their table. "Can I get you guys anything else?"

Gerome shook his head, but Terrance must have been in the mood to be a real shit. "Do you know the guy at the table right over there? Has he ever been in here before?"

She pursed her lips and shook her head. "Not that I can remember. He paid his bill, though, and left a tip in dimes. The guy doesn't have much. He counted out ones for the bill."

"Thanks."

"Do you think he's trouble? Richard did have to get rid of that guy who was with him." She turned to look as Puppy-Dog Eyes got up to leave. "Come to think of it, I doubt it. He's just down on his luck or something. We get folks like that a lot this time of year." She seemed to be settling in for a talk. "It's warmer here, so some people migrate down and live outside or in tents and stuff. I've seen a few places off the key where it's like a tent city with homeless people in the woods."

Gerome only half paid attention as the guy left, and he was tempted to see where he went.

"You want to follow him, don't you?" Terrance asked. "You know, nothing says 'I'm interested in you' like following someone home."

"Look." Gerome set down his beer a little harder than necessary. "This is the guy who was looking for our package. Maybe I can find out something about it." He stood up and handed Terrance some money. "Take care of the bill, and I'll see you later."

Chapter 2

TUCKER WELLS hurried out of the restaurant, looking around the parking lot for the guy from inside. He didn't seem to be around, and Tucker hoped he never saw him again. Forget about the money he promised. Nothing good was going to come of this. It wasn't Tucker's fault that he couldn't find whatever had been dropped overboard, and the more he thought about it, the more he wondered why this guy didn't just look for it himself if it was so important.

He walked to the roadside and looked each way before turning left. It had taken him a while to walk to the restaurant, and now he had to walk back to where he was staying. Tucker moved quickly, trying to put as much distance as possible between that guy and him.

About a block up the road, he paused and turned around. He had the feeling that someone was behind him, but he didn't see anyone. He thought about running, but instead he walked as fast as he could. Tucker didn't hear anything more from behind him, but he continued moving quickly just to be safe.

He passed a couple of shopping centers that were now mostly dark, with just a few lights in the parking lots. His belly grumbled because a single grilled cheese sandwich wasn't enough food. Especially now that his belly had gotten something, it yearned for more. But Tucker had no money and no way to get any. He had been hoping that the man would indeed pay him and he would have a chance to eat and maybe be full for the first time in quite a while.

Still, he had eaten, and he was better off with this guy away from him and out of his life, hopefully for good.

Movement behind him caught his attention and then stilled. Tucker's nerves grew. He was only about a half mile from the camp area where he had been staying, and once he was there, he could hide among the others and everything would be fine. As he approached the turnoff, he checked behind him once again before making the turn down the side street to the small, sparsely wooded area on the other side of the key.

At the edge of the camp, he hurried to his small tent and ducked inside. He had just a few things inside, including some sort-of-clean clothes and his blankets and the pad he used as a mattress. There were also a few bottles of water he had gotten at one of the shelters, and an old Igloo cooler. It was empty now but acted as his refrigerator when he had something to keep inside it.

"Tucker," a small voice said, and he peeked his head out of the tent.

"Hey, Joshie," he said as brightly as he could, his heart still pounding in his ears, even though he should be relatively safe here.

"Mama went to the food bank and got stuff. She made dinner." He held out his hand, and Tucker took it, letting Joshie lead him over to a beat-up picnic table near the larger tent that acted as Joshie's home.

"You haven't been eating," Cheryl Henning, Joshie's mother, said as she set a plastic plate in front of him as soon as he sat down. It was boxed mac and cheese, but it seemed gourmet to his nearly empty stomach. She set down two more plates along with plastic cups of water and then sat down to eat.

"Thank you. I thought I had some work, but it didn't pan out." God, he was reminded of just how close to desperation everyone here was. He'd actually taken a shady job to retrieve something from the beach that could have been drugs or God knows what, and as a result he'd had a run-in with a really shady character. At least he'd gotten away.

"It's okay. We're all used to things not working out," Cheryl said softly and ate what was on her plate. Tucker glanced at Joshie's plate and hers and was grateful they were willing to share what little they had.

The only light they had to see by came from a street-light a ways away and a few lanterns hung throughout the camp. They weren't allowed to build any open fires, so they did what they could to survive.

Tucker waited until they had all finished dinner before handing Joshie some of the shells he had found on the beach.

"These are neat. Thanks, Tucker." Joshie hurried off to put them wherever he kept his treasures.

"I heard a rumor that the police are going to run us all off," Cheryl told him quietly. "I think in the morning we should pack up and move someplace else before we get into trouble." She was already cleaning up her things and placing them in the few plastic tubs that housed their possessions. She had a vehicle, but she rarely used it because gas was too expensive, and Tucker doubted it was even insured. Still, it ran, and maybe they could find another place to camp.

"Okay. I'll be up with the light and we can get the tents down and leave before anyone makes a fuss." There were no rules, and everyone came and went, but it was best to just be gone before anyone began asking questions or caused any trouble.

Cheryl and Joshie weren't his family. Well, they were, of a sort. Tucker had met them about three months ago when the temperatures cooled and he realized he didn't have a permanent place to live. Tucker had joined one of the camp areas outside Tampa, and he'd had the luck to pitch his little tent next to theirs. Cheryl had shown him the ropes, and Joshie had befriended him. No one in the camp had very much, and they seemed to have less than some of the others. A few times Tucker got day jobs, and he shared his good fortune with them. They did the same with him, but Tucker tried not to burden Cheryl. She had Joshie, and he had to come first.

"I'll see both of you in the morning," Tucker said and thanked Cheryl for the meal. Then he said good night to Joshie and went back into his tent, closing the flap for some privacy. Here, in a place like this, privacy was not being seen. It was hard not to be heard, with only canvas walls, and some of the sounds that reached his ears Tucker wished he could unhear and wash out of his memory. What really concerned him was that Joshie could hear those same things—the fights, the name-calling, people coupling in the night. All of it mixed together in a *Humanity's Greatest Hits* album.

In preparation for the morning, Tucker packed up the things he wasn't going to need right away, filling the cooler with his few possessions and putting his extra clothes in an old backpack he had found.

A disturbance from outside the tent—increased activity and a few raised voices—caught his attention, and he stuck his head outside to see a man holding one of the others, ready to punch him. Tucker recognized the man from the restaurant. He must have followed him.

"Where is he? I saw him come into this shithole." He shook Roger, one of the other guys, and Roger pointed in Tucker's direction. The guy dropped Roger as though he were nothing and turned toward Tucker.

Tucker climbed out of the tent. "What do you want?" he asked as the guy strode over as though he owned the world and everyone in it.

"I want what I told you to get for me," he growled, grabbing Tucker's shirt.

"I didn't find anything," Tucker said. "There was nothing there." He looked into this guy's rage-filled eyes and wondered how much of a beating he was going to get before the guy realized Tucker was telling the truth. "I did what you asked and found nothing." He tried to keep his voice level even as he was dragged up onto his toes.

The punch to the gut knocked all the wind out of him, and he crumpled to the ground, coughing and trying to breathe. "Tell me where it is, or I'll tear this place apart to find it."

"I don't know," Tucker croaked. "Maybe out to sea." He braced himself for more pain, maybe a kick or worse, but it didn't happen.

Tucker lifted his gaze as the man fell backward, pulled to the ground without a word. At first Tucker thought the other people around had taken action, but instead a single man centered in his gaze.

"That's enough. You get the hell out of here or I'll snap your neck like a twig." He never raised his voice, but menace filled his soft tone. "I could kill you if I wanted, and I'm sure I would be doing the world a favor."

"Do you know who you're messing with?" the man growled as he tried to get back on his feet.

"Don't care. You need to leave folks alone." Tucker's savior pulled the other man to his feet. A glint of steel caught Tucker's eye, but his savior reacted quickly, grabbing the wrist and forcing the knife to the ground. "Coward." He shoved the other man hard, and he stumbled back the way he came, with Tucker's hero pushing and hounding him until he ended up in the muddy area at the end of the camp. "Now get out of here and stay away from these people." He waited as the mud monster hobbled off.

Tucker had managed to get to his feet, but his belly hurt like hell. At least the pain was lessening and he could breathe once again. He was grateful that he hadn't gotten sick, but his stomach was definitely unhappy.

"Are you okay?" the guy asked as he drew closer, and Tucker recognized him from the restaurant tonight. "Did he hurt you badly?"

"I'm okay," Tucker said softly. "What are you doing here?" Was this guy following him too? Hell, was he waving some sort of sign that he wanted to be followed?

"I was heading home and saw him skulking behind you. I followed because after what I heard at the restaurant, I figured he would pull something like this." He turned toward where the guy had gone. "He won't return for now."

"Are you sure about that?" Tucker asked. The guy was definitely persistent. He was starting to figure out why, and he hoped to hell the guy would leave him alone. Maybe it was a good thing that they were planning to leave in the morning. He could disappear and then figure out what he was going to do.

"Oh yeah. He won't be back right away." He held Tucker's gaze, and a warmth spread through him. When he wasn't fighting Tucker's battles, this guy was hot as hell. Not that this moment was the time for those types of thoughts, but it was hard not to think about it when a pair of intense dark eyes looked into his.

"And if he is, we won't be here anyway," he said softly. "I'm Tucker, by the way, and thank you for helping us."

"Gerome." He smiled and glanced around. "You're leaving?"

Tucker nodded. "We were planning to pack up in the morning. There are some rumors floating around, and we don't want to get caught up in anything. So my friend and her son and I were leaving anyway. Maybe we should have just packed up and gone already."

Gerome nodded. "What did Muscles want, anyway?"

"Something that was supposed to have washed up on the beach. I was looking for it and never found it. He must have thought I took it and was pissed. But I never did, and if it was so important, then he should have gone looking for it himself."

Gerome hummed and glanced around once again. “I’m going to suggest that you all pack up now and put your stuff in whatever vehicle you have. I have an idea that what went down hasn’t gone unnoticed, and it’s likely our friend will try to get his revenge.”

“But where do we go? It’s dark, and Cheryl has a son. I can’t leave her and Joshie.” They helped each other, and Tucker felt bad enough that he had brought trouble to their doorstep. He wasn’t going to leave them to fend for themselves. Life out here was hard enough, but going it alone was even worse.

Gerome blew the air out of his mouth and then angled his gaze skyward as though the stars would provide the answer. Tucker had looked up and wished on them enough to know that they weren’t going to help anyone. “Go ahead and get packed if you can.” He turned away and pulled out his phone, walking through the camp and out toward the road as he talked.

“Do you think this guy is on the level?” Cheryl asked as soon as Gerome was gone. “He’s bigger than the other one, and he tossed that guy around like he was nothing.” Her eyebrows knitted together. “I don’t know if we can trust him.”

Tucker watched Gerome in the light of the streetlamp. “I have no idea what he wants or if he can help at all. Maybe we should just pack up and get out of here. We can probably find a turnoff somewhere and sleep in the car for the rest of the night. Then we can move on.” His gaze barely left Gerome, especially once he’d hung up and strode back.

“I can’t believe I’m doing this, but okay. I have a friend. He and his husband moved in together, and they’re waiting out the lease on their place. It has about six weeks left, and they’re not living there. Go ahead and finish packing, and we'll get you out of here. The three of you can stay there for a few days." He sighed and rolled his eyes, the streetlight glistening in them. "But don't think of trying to pull anything."

"Us?" Tucker hissed in a whisper. "You're the one who's as big as a house."

Gerome nodded. "Just remember that. I'm also the one who saved your skin." He leaned closer. "And to answer your next question, I don't want anything from any of you other than not to cause trouble and to be on your best behavior. Nothing."

"Then why?" Tucker asked.

Gerome groaned softly. "Because I'm fucking Robin Hood. Just get packed, and fast, and don't make me regret doing this. Okay?"

Tucker found himself nodding and wondering if there wasn't more to it than that. But he didn't really have much choice, and Gerome was offering an apartment for them to stay in, even if for just a few days. That meant a real bathroom and shower and a chance to do real laundry rather than rinsing things out in a sink. He turned to Cheryl for her answer, and she nodded slowly. "Yeah."

He wanted to say more but remained quiet. This was almost too good to be true, and that made him suspicious, but what the hell was he going to do? They were getting desperate, and the nights were growing cold, some close to freezing. "Go ahead and pack up. I'll do the same."

Cheryl went back to her tent and began hauling things out before sliding two tubs in the back of the old SUV. Then Cheryl carried out Joshie and laid him on the back seat before taking down her tent. Tucker put his things in the back as well and got his tent down and rolled up in a few minutes, along with his bedding. The area that had been home for the past month barely held any impression that they had been there at all.

Cheryl got into the car and started the engine, which roared to life. Gerome got in the front, and Tucker slid in next to Joshie, taking him in his arms as they slowly pulled off the dirt road and out toward the main street. They got maybe a few blocks before lights appeared down the street, flashing brighter as they grew closer before passing them and turning toward the camp.

"Make a right at the next street," Gerome instructed, and they traveled two blocks down. "Okay, turn here and park right there." Gerome pointed, and Cheryl pulled into the empty space. "This is parking for the unit you're using, so you don't have to worry about moving. I'll open up the unit and give you a key. Bring in your things, but leave the tents out here." He seemed like the kind of guy who liked telling people what to do.

Cheryl got out slowly and lifted Joshie into her arms. He woke up, and she put him on his feet and held his hand as they went inside. The apartment was furnished with boring, serviceable furniture, but it was clean and nice. It smelled dry but was a bit cold. Gerome kicked on the furnace, and it began warming up.

"The futon turns into a bed, and there's a single bedroom down here." He motioned, and Cheryl followed him. "Go ahead and bring in the rest of your stuff. There are a few things in the refrigerator. Help yourself to whatever you need. I'll stop by in the morning to make sure you're okay." He let the words hang in the air. "There's bedding for the futon in the closet.

I live right across the hall." He left and closed the door behind him.

"OH MY God," Cheryl breathed. "What have we done to deserve this?" She took Joshie down the hall and returned wide-eyed. "There's a really nice bathroom with shampoo and soap. Joshie, come on." She disappeared, and Tucker heard water running in the tub. "Let's get you a bath before I put you back to bed." Tucker figured once Joshie was asleep, Cheryl would take her chance to avail herself of the tub as well.

"I'm still wondering what he wants," Tucker said.

"Okay, yeah… but I haven't been clean in so long, I don't know what it feels like." She looked about to cry.

"Use the bathroom. I'll take a turn after you." He just wanted to get clean and then sleep forever. The apartment was warm now, and there was no wind to keep out.

Cheryl took Joshie into the bathroom and closed the door. After a little while, a very tired Joshie came out in a pair of pajamas that were just a little too short and very faded. He gave Tucker a hug good night, and then Cheryl took him into the bedroom. While Cheryl took her turn in the bath, Tucker made up his bed. Then he got in the bathroom once Cheryl was done and had closed the bedroom door.

Tucker set down his clean clothes and stripped down, turned on the water, and stepped under the shower. God, it felt good to be warm, and as he soaped up, the water went from gray to clear. He hadn't realized how dirty he was until he began getting clean. Tucker sighed and closed his eyes, water sluicing over him as he washed his hair. It had been a long time since he'd had a haircut, but it felt so much better clean. When he stepped out, he dried and combed it before pulling on a threadbare T-shirt and shorts.

He cleaned up the bathroom and hung up all the towels before turning out the lights and slipping under the covers. He couldn't suppress a sigh as his skin met fresh sheets, with everything smelling clean. He inhaled deeply just to remind himself what that was like before closing his eyes.

Tucker knew he should be worried about what was to come. No one did something for nothing. But whatever the price was, he could figure out if it was too high. At least for tonight, he was safe, warm, and comfortable, and so were Cheryl and Joshie. That would have to be enough for now.

Chapter 3

"WHAT IN the fuck did you do?" Terrance asked the following morning as he barged into Gerome's apartment. Gerome wasn't even out of bed and he was already being assaulted by one of his best friends. "You put strangers up in Richard's old place? What were you thinking?"

Gerome pushed back the covers and stood naked in front of Terrance, who turned around and left the room.

Gerome threw on a robe, joined Terrance out in his small kitchen, and put the coffee on. "Now, what are you going on about?" He passed Terrance a mug. "You do realize that our friend from the restaurant last night was pressuring people, and it seems Tucker was acting as an unwitting mule."

"So what?"

Gerome smacked him. "Just listen and drink your coffee. I was the one who stopped him from completing his job. It's the brick of money in my closet that's causing him trouble. And the guy, along with his friend and her son, have been living in tents. They're staying in an apartment that Richard is still paying for and was empty, doing nothing. So don't give me a bunch of shit." He was being nice to someone. "Besides, if there's real criminal activity going on around us, that is going to lead to scrutiny, and you know what that means?"

"Oh shit, not again," Terrance groaned. "What is it with you guys? You meet some kid and you start acting all weird."

Gerome finished his coffee and set the mug in the sink. "Forget that. Last night was a drop at sea, and the money brick proves it. That means that illicit activity is happening right out there. It isn't just down by Miami or out on the Keys. If it continues, then the feds and other police are going to be here to try to put a stop to it. Or worse, what if what's left of the Garvic family decides to move in? If it's lucrative, those fuckers will smell the money all the way in Detroit. What if they're already here? We have to find out and put an end to this shit. That means that Tucker across the hall is our one lead right now."

Terrance growled, but Gerome knew he'd already won. "What does Richard say?"

"Who do you think gave me permission last night?" He cocked his eyebrows.

Terrance grimaced. "I think both of you have gone completely soft, each because of a cute pair of eyes and a great ass." He shook his head. "Not that I can blame you on either count, but why does this hotness always come with strings? Can't you just pick up a guy, have some fun, fuck, and then walk away? It's what you used to do. None of this soft, mushy stuff." He slipped off the stool. "Do what you want. Just don't come to me when it all blows up in your face."

That was as close to approval as Gerome was going to get.

"What bug crawled up your ass?" Gerome asked.

"Me?" Terrance set down his mug hard enough that coffee spilled on the counter. "You've been terrible for months, mopey and as snappy as a gator. Now you meet some kid and suddenly—" Terrance paused and rolled his eyes. "You really like this kid...."

"Don't even go there. We need to find out what's going on for our own safety."

Terrance snorted and then did it again as he laughed. "You could do that by scaring the shit out of him until he tells you what you want to know. Don't forget, I saw this guy, and he was cute as all hell. Besides, you don't even know if he walks on our side of the street or not. You said he's with a woman and her kid. Maybe they're involved."

"Like usual, you have it all wrong." Okay, maybe not all of it, because Gerome had spent much of the night wondering about a certain young man. He wasn't going to tell Terrance that every time he closed his eyes, he saw those blue eyes filled with worry. "Now shut it and stop giving me a hard time. It's early and I need to get dressed. I told Tucker I would be over this morning."

A knock on the door had them both turning. Gerome set down his mug, yawned, and pulled open the door.

Richard, Daniel, and Coby came inside, with Daniel looking him over. "Nice robe. Though if you don't want to flash the neighbors, I suggest you go put something else on."

"God," Gerome muttered as he pulled his robe together and stalked off toward the bedroom. "There's coffee—help yourself."

"We will," Daniel said with amusement.

Pans clanged in his kitchen as Gerome closed the bedroom door behind him. Gerome sighed and stripped off his robe, heading to the bathroom to clean up quickly. Then he pulled on jeans and a newer T-shirt, taking a moment to lament the loss of the Detroit shirts he hadn't been able to bring along. When they had entered witness protection, the marshals had gone through everything they owned to make sure there was nothing obvious about their pasts, and they took all his Detroit T-shirts and jerseys. Dammit.

He padded barefoot back out to where Daniel was serving breakfast. He handed Gerome a plate and a refilled mug of coffee. The others stood or sat at the counter snack bar. Gerome sat on the nearby sofa, setting his plate on the coffee table. What he really wanted was to be alone, but it seemed his family wasn't going to allow it.

Daniel sat next to him, Richard and Terrance taking turns making Coby laugh. "Sometimes I don't want to be around other people either."

Gerome shrugged. "Sometimes I wish…." He let his voice trail off because it really didn't matter what he wanted.

"I know. You want your life back," Daniel said softly. "But did you ever stop to think that if you got your wish, that your life, the one you had before…

wouldn't fit now. You can't tell me that Gerome Meadows could return and seamlessly fit into those shoes again? You aren't that same person. And do you know how I know that?" Daniel had this way of asking a few questions and making Gerome seem really stupid.

"You're going to say because of what I did yesterday in helping Tucker and Cheryl. But it isn't like that. There's something going on that could affect all of us, and we need to find out what it is."

Daniel patted him on the shoulder. "You keep telling yourself that." He stood and went back over to Coby, who climbed off his stool and hurried over before plopping himself down next to Gerome.

"Mr. Gerome…," Coby said with a grin.

"Hey…."

"I saw your penis," Coby said in a singsong way and then broke out into a fit of giggles.

Gerome looked up at the ceiling and then broke into an embarrassed smile. God, flashing a four-year-old hadn't been intentional at all.

"Coby, we don't talk that way. Now come back over here and finish your breakfast. Gerome and Terrance need to talk to Richard, and we're going to go to the park to play."

Coby bounded down, and Richard lifted him back onto the stool.

Gerome ate a few bites of eggs and realized how hungry he was, then finished off the food in a hurry. He put his dishes in the dishwasher and gathered the rest of them as well. Daniel and Coby said goodbye. "We'll be back in about half an hour." Daniel left with Coby, and Gerome turned to the other two.

"Let's talk about what you saw last night," Richard said.

"It was an offshore meeting." He left and returned with the plastic-encased bundle. "I heard them yelling, and later I found this in the surf. I've been able to put together that Tucker, the guy staying in your old place, was supposed to try to find it. He didn't. I did."

Richard picked it up, peering through the wrapped layers. "I can't tell what it is."

"Terrance thinks it's cash," Gerome supplied.

"Too light for drugs. That much would weigh a lot more." He reached over and tilted the block. "You can see a head right there."

Richard nodded. "Okay. So we believe what we have is drug money. What do we do with it?"

Gerome picked up the block and carried it to the other room, hiding it once again.

"Nothing. That isn't our problem right now. Drug running right off the key is the problem. Now, we did see someone who's involved. The guy you kicked out of the bar last night. Anyone recognize him?" Gerome asked.

"No. I got a good look at him and I'd know him again, but he wasn't familiar. But you're right. We need to try to find out who he is and who he might work for so we can get them the hell out of here." Richard slowly began to pace the floor. "We can't let on to our friends across the hall who we are. But we have to find out what we can." He turned to Gerome. "You saved this guy, so he has to feel some sort of gratitude. Be nice to him and see what he'll tell you. Find out where he met the guy and what exactly he was supposed to do. There may be some sort of information we can use."

"Is that all?" Gerome asked.

"What do you want to do?" Richard had definitely changed after meeting Daniel. He seemed much more settled and calm. The angst and longing that Gerome felt, that he used to see in Richard, were gone. "Be honest, do you like this guy?"

Gerome shrugged. He wasn't sure what he felt, or what he had a right to feel.

"You know it's okay to like someone. We have to be careful, but there's no reason why you can't try to be happy."

Gerome wanted to scream. "I don't know how to be happy here. I've tried, but it's so damned boring. I spend every day helping boring tourists pick out the same boring geegaw, and smile and do what I'm supposed to. I hate it. I want to be free like we were then. We ran the show; we did what we wanted. If someone crossed us, they sure as hell didn't do it again. The three of us had power, we were somebodies.... Now we're nobodies."

He sat down. That was a lot more than he'd intended to say. "I know we can't go back, but that doesn't mean I don't want to." He bit his lower lip and raised his gaze. "For fuck's sake, I saw them last night and had to help them. They were living in tents with a kid the same age as Coby. What the hell was I supposed to do?"

Richard gazed at him indulgently. "You know you did what Mom would do. What she would want us to do," Richard told him softly.

Gerome found himself nodding. Both he and Richard had grown up in foster care and on the streets. Of the three of them, only Terrance had had a real parent, his mom. And she had taken the rest of them into her heart. Terrance's mother had been mom to all three of them, and Gerome had loved her. They all did. So much so that when, after going into protection, they found out she wasn't going to last much longer, they'd broken security to be able to say goodbye. It had been a unanimous decision.

"Yeah, I guess," he begrudgingly agreed. "I should go on over and see that they're okay and shit. Make sure they haven't walked off with everything that isn't nailed down."

"I'm going home to get ready for work," Terrance announced and left without saying anything more.

"What's with him?" Richard asked.

"He's angry with me for bringing them here." Gerome saw Richard to the door. "I wish I understood it."

Richard clapped him on the shoulder. "Give him a chance. If you're feeling lost, then I bet he is too… as we all are." He caught Gerome's gaze. "Nothing is ever perfect, and the changes we've been through have taken a toll on us."

"You have Daniel and Coby," Gerome said.

"Yes, and they make me happy. But that doesn't erase the fact that I sometimes wish for what I had. I love Daniel and Coby with everything I have, but sometimes I wish things were still the same. I won't hurt them, so I accept what I have to and try to move forward. We ran a large organization in Detroit, and now I mix drinks and own part of a business. It's not anything like what we had before, but I guess it's enough."

"What are you saying?"

"I don't think we can have everything we might want. But find something to make you happy. Something that's enough for you."

"Is Daniel only enough?" Gerome asked.

Richard shook his head. "Daniel is everything. So enough is just that. It's good enough because I have him. He makes it all better." He pulled open the door. "You're my brother, and I want you—both of you—to be content." He left the apartment, and Gerome figured he might as well pay his morning visit before getting ready for work.

He followed Richard out and knocked on the door across the hall. It was opened a minute later by Tucker, with a little boy half hidden behind him. They still seemed to be in sleep clothes, with the boy in faded pajamas, munching on some crackers. "Yes, we're still here, and we didn't steal anything," Tucker said.

Gerome decided to let that go for now. "Did you get some rest? Do you have what you need?"

Tucker nodded. "Thank you for letting us stay. Cheryl is still sleeping, and once she gets up, we'll be on our way. It was very nice of you to let us clean up and stuff."

The washing machine began to spin, and Gerome quickly figured out what they had been doing. "Stay for a few days and get yourselves together and rested. I have to go to work in a little while. But when I get back, I was hoping to talk with you."

"About?" Tucker asked, folding his arms over his chest. Man, this guy might not be big, but the determination and spirit inside him were probably why he survived on the streets. His eyes grew darker with suspicion, and Gerome found himself getting a little lost in them for a split second.

He thought of just saying what he wanted, but he held back. "About what happened to you." He stepped closer. "I'm not a jerk, you know, and you don't need to treat me like one. I was good to you, but I'm not looking for anything from you. So being defensive isn't necessary."

"Oh yeah?" Tucker raised his eyebrows, but his posture relaxed a little. "When you haven't had anything to live in other than a tent, people tend to think they can take advantage or abuse you. The cops raided what had been our home yesterday, and only because we don't have any other place to go. Did it look like we were making a mess? That camp area was clean."

Gerome didn't argue. "So what do you want me to do? Act like an ass so your expectations will be fulfilled?"

Cheryl shuffled into the room. "Tucker," she said softly. She looked pale and drawn, more so than she had the night before.

"Do you want something to eat?" Gerome asked, but she shook her head. "I have some juice over at my place. I'll bring it over for you." Cheryl smiled and went back in the bedroom. "Let me get the juice. You'll need to watch over her if she's sick."

"I make Mommy better," Joshie said and hurried back to the bedroom.

"Keep him away from her as much as possible in case it's the flu or something. I'll stop by the drugstore on my way home from work for medicine and stuff."

Gerome went back to his place, grabbed the orange juice, and took it to Tucker, along with a loaf of bread, some lunch meat, and mayonnaise. All three of them were so thin that he wanted to make sure that they ate. "Stay inside if you can in case the guy from yesterday is looking for you, and I'll be back once I'm done with work."

Gerome left and closed the door behind him. Then he headed to work, wondering why he kept seeing Tucker's confused disbelief flashing in his mind the entire time.

"YES, OF course I can wrap that for you," Gerome said and pulled open the drawer of tissue to wrap up a four-dollar purchase as though it came from Tiffany's. He was never going to get used to the entitlement. "There you are." He gave the woman a bag and smiled again as the lady left.

The store had had a surprisingly busy day. Gerome had anticipated that business would fall off to nothing after Christmas, but it seemed that enough people came here to escape the winters up north that business was holding pretty steady.

"Are you closed?" a man in his forties asked as he hurried inside. "I need a present for my wife's birthday, and I have half an hour. Any ideas?" He seemed frantic.

Gerome took pity on him, showing him some nice handmade handbags, a few printed silk scarves, and a pair of amethyst earrings from the case. The guy must have been desperate, because he bought one of the bags, two scarves, and the earrings, handing Gerome the credit card. Gerome rang everything up, wrapped each item separately with different color ribbon so the customer was happy, and sent him on his hurried way. Then he closed the store, prepared the deposit, and walked to the bank to drop the bag in the night drop before heading for home.

He always felt better once the money was out of his hands. Gerome never felt the need to steal from the store. That wasn't his style. In Detroit, he and the others had skimmed a good deal of money out of the clubs they ran and transferred it offshore into numbered accounts for each of them. He had always viewed it as their retirement funds. But that was totally different. The money flowing into the clubs wasn't legitimate in the first place… at least most of it wasn't. This little business was, and besides, petty larceny was way beneath him.

"The store is closed, and I dropped the deposit at the bank," he told Betty on the phone as he walked to his car. "It was a good day."

"That's wonderful," she said. "The customers just love you."

Gerome smiled. "I sold another of those handmade purses." Betty made them herself, and Gerome knew it made her happy whenever one sold. "Bring in a few more when you get a chance."

"Oh, I will," she said happily. "I'll see you tomorrow with them when I stop by." She hung up, and Gerome put his phone away. He stopped in at the drugstore before going the rest of the way home.

He knocked on the apartment door, and Tucker answered with Joshie once again behind him.

"I got some cold and flu stuff for Cheryl and a few goodies for this guy." A cough reached his ears from the other room. "How is she?"

"She's coughing and sleeping a lot, but she's eaten and says she feels better." Tucker stepped back, and Gerome entered. The apartment was even cleaner than it had been that morning. Gerome reached into the bag and handed Joshie a box of animal crackers. He ran off with them, climbing onto the sofa holding the box as though it were some sort of prize. Gerome smiled as he watched him, wondering at the situation when so simple a gift had brought such an expression of excitement.

"Do you want something to drink? I have water and some of the juice you brought earlier," Tucker said, closing the door behind them.

"I'm fine," Gerome told him and sat at the snack bar. "I need you to answer a few questions for me."

Tucker sat down. "Are you a cop or something? Is that how you knew to help us get out of the camp last night?" he asked, picking up a napkin and twisting it in his fingers.

"No. I'm not a cop. I work at a gift shop down the road." Gerome wondered how he could get to what he needed.

"Then who are you and why do you know what's happening?" Tucker asked.

Gerome knew he had to be more careful. He had assumed since Tucker had agreed to find that package that Tucker was naïve, but maybe he had just been desperate.

"Doesn't matter, does it?" He leaned closer. "This is a nice community, relatively quiet, with vacationers, some locals, and seasonal people. They come here because it's quiet and peaceful. No one wants shady things to happen here." *They* certainly didn't.

"What about the police?" Tucker asked. "Won't they help?"

Gerome met his gaze. "Do you want to call them and explain what happened?" He already knew that answer. Tucker and his friends wanted to stay under the radar just as much as Gerome did. That was pretty obvious. Not that they had done anything wrong, in Gerome's opinion, but indigents were targets, easily manipulated and abused simply because they were vulnerable. "I didn't think so. Can you tell me what this guy looked like? A really good description. I only saw him at the bar and last night." That wasn't the total truth, but maybe Tucker had noticed something Gerome hadn't.

"He was smarmy. Both times I saw him he was in expensive clothes. I was down at the marina looking for cans to recycle so I could get some money to buy a little bread for Joshie when he pulled up in an Audi. He asked if I wanted to earn some money. He handed me a few bills and told me what he wanted and where to meet him. Said I was to bring the package to the bar and he could give me three hundred dollars." Tucker shook a little. "I knew I was probably getting into something shady, but it was a lot of money that could feed the three of us for a month or more." He lowered his voice. "Do you know what it sounds like when a five-year-old is going to bed hungry?"

Gerome did know. He had done exactly that many times when he was a kid, and yeah, it was terrible. "So you were desperate."

Tucker shrugged. "There aren't many opportunities for upward mobility in a tent camp, are there? Of course I was desperate. I still am. The only reason we have a roof right now is because of you."

Joshie laughed, and Gerome realized he was watching cartoons, shoveling the crackers into his mouth.

Tucker turned and smiled himself. "God, that's a beautiful sound." He shifted his attention back to Gerome.

"Do you know what was in the bundle you were supposed to find?" Gerome asked.

"No. All I know was that if I brought it to him at the bar, he would pay me, and that I wasn't supposed to look inside. That's all. I figured it was probably drugs or something, but I don't know. I figured I would get it, hide it somewhere, and then tell the guy at the bar where it was and that would be it. The less I handled it or was seen with it, the better."

Gerome nodded. "I suspect our friend is going to be looking for his package pretty closely, and he isn't going to give up very easily." What he didn't understand was why the guy didn't just go get it himself, unless he was afraid there might be someone else after it, or that the police might get involved. If Tucker got caught, he'd know nothing, and the operation would be safe. That was the only reasoning Gerome could come up with.

"Okay. What else do you all need?" Gerome asked as a firm knock sounded on the door. Tucker tensed, and Gerome had him join Joshie before he checked who was outside the door. Then he opened it for Daniel and Coby.

"I brought a few things for our guests," Daniel said as he came inside with a huge smile.

"Tucker, Joshie, this is my friend Daniel, and this is Coby." The little guy had already hurried over to Joshie to say hello and ask if he liked to play trucks. It seemed Joshie did, because they both settled on the floor in front of the television, and Coby opened the bag he had been carrying and spread out the toys.

"I brought some things for Joshie. I hope that's okay, and I have a few things for the refrigerator as well as some clothes for your lady friend." He handed over the bundle of clothes and a bag of toiletries and other items. "And there are gift cards for the grocery store and for Target. It's just up the street that way."

Tucker took the things, his hands shaking a little. "Thank you," he said softly.

Gerome figured he was a little overwhelmed and wasn't used to this kind of generosity. It wasn't something in his wheelhouse of experiences either, but Daniel was nothing like most of the people he had encountered in his life.

Daniel was a rare person who had flirted with the dark side of the law and life and had pulled himself back from the brink. He had been a hacker in college—a quite accomplished one if Gerome understood correctly. But he'd given it up and gone into the other side of the business. Daniel was talented, smart, and had a heart of gold.

"How is your friend?" Daniel asked.

"Mama's sick," Joshie said.

"Okay." Daniel stood and went down the hall. He knocked on the door and explained softly who he was before going inside.

"Is he a doctor or nurse or something?" Tucker asked, tensing.

Gerome shook his head. "He's a father. Sometimes I swear there isn't anything Daniel can't do."

Daniel came back in the room, got some juice, and handed it to Tucker. "Take this to her and then see if you can get her up and into the shower," he told Tucker. "She'll probably feel better." He dug through the bag of things Gerome had bought for her at the drug store. "And these might help."

Joshie hurried over and leaned against Tucker. "Can you make Mama better?"

"We're gonna try," Daniel said gently. "Your mama needs to sleep, so you have to be quiet. Can you do that for her?" he asked, and Joshie nodded really seriously before returning to where he and Coby had been playing and relaying to Coby that they had to be quiet. The two boys whispered after that as they played—sometimes some very intense whispering. But it was adorable, and Gerome couldn't help smiling.

"Let me take this to her, and I'll see what else Cheryl needs." Tucker went down the hall with the glass and pills, and Daniel shook his head.

"What's wrong with her?" Gerome asked.

"I don't know. She seems completely worn out. I suspect that she's been running on every reserve of energy her body could produce, and now that she's somewhere safe, it's catching up with her. I'd give her a day or two, no more. If she isn't better, then we need to get her to a doctor. But for now, let her rest." He patted Gerome's shoulder. "You're doing a good thing here."

Gerome glared at Daniel, who smiled mischievously back at him.

"Fine. I won't tell anyone that there's a heart buried under all that bravado and prickliness. I wouldn't want to ruin your reputation as a pain in the ass. But it's still nice what you're doing."

Gerome leaned close. "I'm doing this because I need to protect all of us, and that means you and Coby too. If bad elements start to move in here, we could be discovered. The world is a lot smaller than any of us thinks most of the time. If these elements get a real foothold here, then that will draw more, which means additional criminal eyes, money, police activity, and a bigger chance that the pasts we're trying to bury will be resurrected." He tried to hit Daniel with his coldest stare, but it didn't do a damned bit of good. It never did with Daniel. He just stared back for a second, shook his head, and then smiled indulgently.

"If you say so." He patted Gerome on the shoulder once again and stood as Tucker came back toward them.

"Cheryl drank most of the juice and took the pills. She is going to get up and shower. She also said she was hungry." The relief in Tucker's eyes was palpable.

"That's good." Daniel slipped off his stool. "Coby, we need to go."

"Okay." Coby began picking up the toys. "You can have this one and this one," he said, handing the two trucks to Joshie. "Now you can play trucks any time you want." He put the rest of the toys into his bag. "I gotta go. But we can play later if you want."

Joshie nodded and held the two toys like they were the greatest gifts he had ever received. "Thank you."

Daniel and Coby left, and Gerome figured he might as well too. "I should go."

Tucker stood behind the snack bar in the kitchen, rinsing out the dishes. "Look, you're the reason we're here and have anything right now. The least I can do is cook for you if you want to have dinner with us." He put the now clean glasses back in the cupboard.

"You don't have to," Gerome said as Tucker pulled open the refrigerator and got out some of the eggs, meat, and vegetables.

Tucker smiled as he began prepping and chopping. "Do you know how long it's been since I've had anything fresh? Most of what we eat comes out of a box because things like mac and cheese are super cheap and filling." He set down the knife. "I haven't had an egg like this in so long I barely remember what they taste like." He tried to smile, but it seemed to pause on his lips.

"Can I ask how you came to be… like this?" Gerome wasn't quite sure how to ask the question and faltered. He never did that. What was happening to him?

"Well, things just fell apart. I worked in kitchens and stuff like that. For a while I had a place, but I never made much money, and I got behind on the rent because I got sick and wasn't able to work. I thought I could make it up and took extra shifts. But the restaurant closed and I was out of a job, and as soon as the landlord heard about it, he kicked me out. After that I didn't have an address and couldn't get another job, and

I was out on my own." He blinked a few times and then went back to chopping. "It shocked me just how fast it happened."

"What did you do?" Gerome asked, sitting on one of the stools, watching the knife as it moved in a blur, Tucker cut so fast.

"That was almost a year ago. I found the tent at a garage sale and ended up in one of the camps because I had no other place. I've managed some day jobs, but without an address, I can't get a real job. So I'm stuck. I've tried to work, but all anyone sees is my threadbare clothes, and when they realize I'm homeless, they turn their back because… I don't know… maybe they think I'm going to ask to camp out in their kitchen or something." He got out a pan, and soon the kitchen filled with the scent of sautéing vegetables, onion, and a little garlic. Damn, the scent was intoxicating. Almost as much as the intensity in Tucker's eyes when his gaze met Gerome's. For a few seconds, Gerome's thoughts wandered off what they were talking about to Tucker's lips before snapping back to what Tucker was saying.

"Huh?" Gerome asked when he realized he had lost the train of the conversation.

"I was saying that not having a home isn't a disease." Gerome followed Tucker's gaze to where Joshie was playing on the floor. "What did he ever do to not deserve a home? But some people think we're the modern-day version of lepers or something. That if they get too close or work with us, somehow they'll be tainted with the same affliction." Tucker set down the knife with a bang and breathed heavily. "People don't even know that so many people in this country live paycheck to paycheck. The loss of a job combined with a little bad luck, and they could be where I am right now.

Through no fault of their own." He stared, and Gerome nodded and sighed softly. "Anyway… that's enough of my complaining." He set the vegetables aside and cracked the eggs, then added a little water and whisked them before wiping out the pan and pouring a small amount of the egg mixture into it with just a few of the vegetables. He scrambled the eggs, cooking them through, and then called Joshie, who hurried over and accepted the eggs with a smile. He blew on them before taking each small bite.

"What would you like?" Tucker asked.

"Whatever you're making," Gerome answered, a little in awe at Tucker's skills.

Tucker knew what he was doing in a kitchen, and the omelet he set in front of Gerome was fluffy, smooth, and tasty as all hell. Cheryl joined them just after Gerome took his first bite. She sat next to Joshie and ate a small amount.

"I'm finally feeling a little better," she said after eating about half of her dinner. "I'm so grateful to you for letting us stay here." She reached out and patted Gerome's hand. "You have no idea how good that bed feels."

"How long had you been living in the tent?"

"Eighteen months. This is the second winter, which isn't so bad. It's the summers with the heat you can't escape that are hardest. We can pitch the tent in the shade, which helps, but you can't keep the heat out no matter what you do. And at night it doesn't cool down, so all you have is heat upon heat." She drank some water and some more juice. "I used to walk Joshie to a shopping center just so we could wander the stores and he could have a chance to cool off and sleep. Most days I'd get him inside and he would fall asleep in the bottom of the cart because he couldn't sleep at night very much." A tear ran down her cheek, and she sniffled a little. "Sometimes I don't know what we're going to do. Joshie is going to need to start school soon, and he deserves a chance at stability. We can't seem to stay anywhere for very long. I do the best I can for him, but I know it isn't enough."

Gerome had no idea what to say. *Work harder, try harder.* Those words came to his lips, but he stopped them. He might have said them a few years ago, but he didn't think that way anymore. The words that threatened to come were some old reflex that just bubbled up. Instead, he said some of the hardest things he had ever uttered. "I don't know what to say. I don't have any answers." The truth was that Gerome's adult life had been about making what he wanted a reality, and if someone got in the way, they were either moved or eliminated. It was that simple. This was something he couldn't move or change, and neither could they.

Tucker, Cheryl, and Joshie were caught in a trap Gerome could see pretty clearly now. When he and the guys had been part of the Garvic organization, they had a piece of the action. They were members of a family. If someone messed with them, they were messing with the entire family. Each of the guys had the others' backs. That was how things worked and how Gerome had lived so much of his life. These three had no one to watch out for them. They were a small unit against a much stronger world, with nothing to fight back with. Which sucked.

"I know you need an address to try to work, so use this one. At least you can get mail here for a while," he offered.

"You've been so nice to us—to Joshie and me—but I can't impose on you and your generosity," Cheryl said.

"What does it cost to use an address?" Gerome countered. "If you can work, then you can try to help yourself." That made perfect sense to him.

"Tucker can work. He's got skills. I don't, and what can I do with Joshie when I'm working? I can't take him with me, and I can't leave him alone. Childcare costs as much as rent sometimes." She sighed. "I'm sorry. I shouldn't be burdening you with my problems. You're only trying to help, and I'm grateful. I really am." She put her hand over her mouth as she started coughing, deep and rattling in her chest.

"Go back to bed and rest for a while. Joshie is fine out here with us," Tucker offered, and she slipped off the stool.

"What's all this?" she asked, seeing the pile of clothes on the other chair.

"A friend brought those for you to see if you could use them," Gerome told her, biting his lower lip. "You have no idea how hard what I'm about to tell you is, but don't let pride stand in the way of some help." Gerome had let pride guide him more than once, and it usually sent him down a damned rabbit hole, even though he was loath to admit it.

Her eyes cleared and she seemed to see him in detail. "You know that's a lot harder to do than it seems."

Gerome nodded. "Tell me about it, sister."

She left the room without saying anything more, and Gerome took her silence for assent.

"How did you come to live here?" Tucker asked as he finished his own dinner. Joshie had cleaned his plate and was back on the floor playing with the trucks.

That was complicated and contained information Gerome couldn't discuss. "I got tired of the cold up north. I always hated winter, and the guys felt the same way, so we headed down here and got jobs on the key. Some friends helped us with the apartments and had some connections." He didn't need to mention that the friends were the US Marshals and that the connections were the witness protection system. None of that could be mentioned at all.

"Do you like it?" Tucker asked.

Gerome found himself shrugging. "The summers are beastly hot, and I don't know a lot of people here." Nothing at all was like it was back in Detroit. "But my friends are here with me. We all moved together, so I suppose that's one bright spot. And the winters are a lot nicer. It's been chilly here the last few days, but it's downright miserable up north." He shrugged. There wasn't much to talk about, and complaining did no good. There was little he could change, and frankly, if they messed things up here, he was certain the marshals would move them to a place in remote Alaska or God knew where.

"I suppose it's best to be grateful for what you have. It could always be worse," Tucker said. The notion struck Gerome as strangely insightful. Tucker had a hell of a lot less than he did, and yet he seemed to look at his situation in a more positive way than Gerome did. Maybe he should work with what he had rather than rail against what he didn't.

Tucker gathered up the plates, rinsed them, and put them in the sink. "I should probably leave you to what you need to do." Gerome knew that was what should happen, but he liked talking to Tucker and spending time with him. There was something about his resilience and fortitude that struck a chord with Gerome. Not to mention the fact that he was adorably cute. When it came to guys, Gerome didn't really have a type—at least he didn't think so; the guys thought he did—but Tucker's intense blue eyes were making him rethink that. Maybe he had a thing for cute guys who seemed a little lost. No, that wasn't it. What attracted him more than anything else was the intensity, the backbone that pushed its way forward, even under insecurity and adversity. That was damned attractive, but Gerome didn't even know if Tucker was interested in him.

What in the hell was he thinking about? Gerome couldn't get involved with anyone. He wasn't Richard, and what were the odds of two of them finding someone who would understand their predicament and keep their mouth shut? Richard had gotten fortunate on top of lucky with Daniel. Gerome had no illusions that he would ever get that kind of opportunity. He had to keep his mouth shut, and the others as well. The exposure of their secret could put all of them at risk. No matter how he felt about this place, he had to keep all three of them safe.

He lifted his gaze after looking away as if to keep his thoughts private, and the momentary heat in Tucker's eyes blew all of those thoughts out of his head. Gerome could lose himself in his eyes just as easily as he got lost sometimes in the blue of the water as he stood near the waves. He swallowed and said good night to both Tucker and Joshie, thanked them for dinner, and then left the apartment.

He closed the door to his home behind him only to have it open and Terrance breeze inside. "Did you find out anything?"

"Unfortunately not. He doesn't know who the man who hired him was, and he played on Tucker's desperation the way we feared. I think we're going to have to be watchful for further activity."

"And what about the package in your closet? We have to do something with it. We aren't to be involved in any illegal activity, and being in possession of that money is very illegal."

Gerome smiled and shrugged. "How so? I didn't do anything to get it other than pick it up off the beach. I can get rid of it quickly if the need arises, but...." He was about to continue when a knock interrupted him. His apartment was turning into Grand Central Station.

Gerome opened the door and Richard came in with a six-pack of beer, which he settled on the counter.

"You may as well start at the beginning," Terrance groused before grabbing a beer and flopping into one of the chairs. "He didn't find out anything, and we were talking about the package in his closet." He tipped the bottle to his lips. "I told him he should get rid of it."

"Why haven't you?" Richard asked.

"I think we need to try to locate these people, and that bundle may be needed as bait. The thing is, I don't want it just landing in their laps. If they've lost that much cash, then that's a pretty expensive cost of doing business. Maybe they'll pick somewhere else the next time." Gerome grinned.

"Then what do we do?" Terrance muttered.

"We watch without looking like we're watching," Gerome explained. "You'll hear things at the bar because news concentrates there. Both of you. I'll watch after Tucker, and—"

Terrance snickered. "I see the way you want to watch him, all right."

"Stop being an ass," Richard told him without malice. "So he likes the kid. There's nothing wrong with that."

"Says the guy who already has someone…." Terrance finished the beer and asked for another one.

Gerome handed him one. "Is that what this Grumpy Bear routine is about? You're jealous?" What the hell was Gerome supposed to do with that? "I can understand, I guess." He grinned. "Who wouldn't be jealous of me?"

Richard preened, and Gerome took a swipe at him, missing by a mile, but at least the tension was broken.

"Can we get past this?" Richard asked, pointedly looking at Gerome.

"With enough beer I can get by anything," Terrance quipped, and Gerome smacked his leg. "Okay, let's do this thing." He lifted his current bottle as a sort of salute. "What are we doing?"

"You both saw the man at the bar…."

"Yeah, the one making trouble for Puppy-Dog Eyes." He snickered, and Gerome wondered just how much Terrance had already had to drink. "I mean Tucker."

"Terrance, knock it off," Richard snapped more forcefully than Gerome had heard him in a while. "This is a danger to all of us."

Terrance shrugged. "No, it's not. It's some guys doing what the fuck they want to do, and it has shit-all to do with us. We lie low, live our lives, and should stay out of it. But we can't, because Gerome has the hots for Tucker and he's already interfered. So now we're involved, Tucker is living across the hall, and Gerome is making eyes at him the same way you were with Daniel." He finished the second beer, belched like a sailor, and eyed the next one before pushing it slightly away.

"What the hell are we? I don't get it. We should bust open that bundle of money, use it to make ourselves a little more comfortable, and spend the fuck out of it. We can save our paychecks, and no one is going to think twice about it."

"What if it's not real?" Richard asked. "What if this is worse than drugs—counterfeiting?" He held his head. "It's trouble, and we need to figure out what's happening on our doorstep." He stood and stalked over to Terrance. "Like it or not, this is our home. Both of you. We have to keep the shit off our turf. Period." He turned and seemed almost haunted. "Do you want to be relocated? I sure as hell don't."

"You have a family now," Terrance muttered. "Of course you don't." He reached for the beer, and Richard stopped him.

Richard leaned nearer, sliding his hand around the back of Terrance's neck, drawing him closer. "I always had a family, you big asshole." He held Terrance's gaze and then turned to Gerome, pulling him closer too. "We were a family, and we still are. It's just gotten a little bigger." He hit Gerome with his no-nonsense stare. "This is our home, and we will protect it."

Chapter 4

TUCKER DIDN'T quite know what to make of Gerome and his friends. There was something about him that made Tucker nervous. Gerome carried himself like he owned the world. The guy had plenty of confidence, and he definitely had the physical power to back it up. Tucker had seen him in action.

"What do you think we should do?" Cheryl asked as she shuffled out of the bedroom the following morning, pulling Tucker out of the thoughts that had plagued him the entire night. Joshie was sound asleep on the sofa, and Tucker stretched his back. He had thought it best to let Joshie sleep away from Cheryl in case she was contagious. "These people seem nice enough and all, but I don't know how much we can trust them." She sat down in the chair with a sigh.

Tucker pushed away the blanket and got up off the thin pad that he usually used in the tent. "I don't think we have much choice but to trust them for now." If Cheryl decided to leave, he couldn't stop her, though he would miss both her and Joshie. As much as he had been determined not to get involved with anyone, the three of them had developed into an unconventional family. "They've been good to us, and they haven't asked us for anything."

She nodded, and Tucker opened the refrigerator. He poured a couple glasses of juice. "I'm glad you're feeling better," he said softly, sitting on the stool next to her.

"The one guy came in the room with me the other day. My head is a little fuzzy on the time line," she said.

"Yeah. His name is Daniel, and he's a friend of Gerome's. He's the one who brought the extra clothes, and his son gave Joshie the trucks." They rested at the foot of the sofa because Joshie had wanted to sleep with them, and they'd compromised. "He also brought by some more food yesterday, and his son played with Joshie." Cheryl had been kind of out of it for a while. "I hope that was okay. I didn't want to disturb you too much. You were sleeping pretty hard a lot of the time."

Cheryl looked much less drawn, and some color had returned. "I appreciate all the help—I do. I was so sick." She set her glass on the counter and turned away. "And you looked after Joshie for me. I've…." A tear ran down her cheek. "I'm lucky you were here when I couldn't be."

"The people helping us were here too. They brought medicine for you and everything," Tucker explained.

Cheryl shook her head. "They want something. That's the only explanation. No one does all of this for nothing, not to help a stranger." Her eyes grew hard. "I wish I knew what it was."

"Gerome is very interested in the man he took out at the campground. I'm not sure why, and his explanation was pretty nebulous, but he did save my butt, and he and his friends were really kind to Joshie. So while I agree with you, I also tend to give them the benefit of the doubt." Something about Gerome told Tucker that he could believe it when he said that he didn't want anything.

"Have you checked on the car?" Cheryl asked. "I don't have valid plates, and…."

"Someone covered it up in the spot, so the plates aren't visible." He shrugged. "I get the feeling these people know what they're doing."

"Do you think they're criminals?" Cheryl asked.

Tucker chuckled. "Living here? I asked if they were police because I thought they might be undercover. But it doesn't seem so. And why would criminals work in a hardware store, a bar, and a gift shop? Here? It doesn't add up." He finished his juice as Joshie stirred and got off the sofa, shuffling to Cheryl, still half asleep.

"I'm hungry, Mommy," he said softly. "Want some juice."

"I'll get you some," Tucker said. "Do you want a piece of toast with jam?" He pulled open the refrigerator to start getting breakfast together.

"Did they bring all that?" Cheryl asked.

"Yes."

A knock startled him slightly. He checked and answered the door. "Hey, Gerome." He smiled and got one in return, which made his belly flutter a little.

"Morning. Do you guys need anything? I have to stop at the store after work and thought I'd ask." His gaze shifted from Tucker to Cheryl. "I see you're feeling better."

"Is Coby coming to play?" Joshie asked.

"I'm not sure," Gerome answered.

"I think we're good," Tucker told him.

Cheryl slipped off the stool and approached Gerome. She stood in front of him, and it looked like the two of them were trying to stare each other down for a second. "Jesus…," she breathed softly. "I've known plenty of men in my time, but you're the stoniest, most closed-off one I have ever met." She didn't look away for another thirty seconds at least.

"What was that for?" Gerome asked.

She finished her juice, and Tucker started a pot of coffee. God, he had missed the stuff. "Sometimes I can read people, but I can't get anything from you. So either you have nothing to hide, or you don't want anyone to possibly see anything."

Tucker had never seen her like this.

"Does that scare you?" Gerome asked.

Cheryl shrugged. "Nope. I worry about people who fidget. You held my gaze. I don't think we have anything to fear from you. But you could bring danger along with you. I'm not sure what to make of that." She stepped away and sat back down, her doubts seemingly satisfied.

"I have to get to work." Gerome seemed a little uncomfortable, and he hurried to the door. "Oh, before I go. Richard—he's the bartender at the Driftwood—said that they were looking for someone to help in the kitchen. I told him you had skills, and he said for you to come on by. If you're interested, he can see about a job."

Tucker could hardly believe it. "Sure. What time does he want me there?" He hadn't thought about how having a job would make him feel. He could be useful again and not take handouts.

"He said to come about eleven. Richard said that they need someone who would help with the prep work and work through the lunch hour." Gerome raised his gaze. "Andi, one of Richard's servers, is saying that she needs help. Cheryl, have you ever waited tables?"

She rolled her eyes. "I've done just about anything."

"Then you could come in with him as well. It's just a few shifts a week, but it might help. Daniel has said that Joshie could come over to play with Coby when you're working. Daniel works from home."

Cheryl's mouth hung open. "Okay. Where did you come from?" Tucker was wondering the same thing. Was this hard, jagged-edged man really some sort of angel in disguise? "You can't be real. No one does this for someone else."

Gerome had his hand on the doorknob, but he turned his gaze to Joshie. "Look, I wasn't all that much older than Joshie when I lost my parents. There was one person who helped me, the mother of one of my friends. She gave me all the care and love I had missed from others. I wasn't her son or even her foster son. But she took the place of my mother and asked nothing in return." Gerome's voice broke. Tucker went to him but hesitated. He wanted to comfort him but didn't have the right and wasn't sure if Gerome would accept it from him. So instead of taking his hand, he just stood there watching him, catching his gaze for a few fleeting seconds. Suddenly Gerome's edges didn't seem as rough, and Tucker realized he was seeing something very rare. "I'm only repaying the kindness that I was shown once." He pulled open the door, and Tucker saw the hard shell fall back into place, jagged edges and all. "Don't make me regret it."

He left, and Tucker stared at the door for a few seconds.

He had to wonder what all that was about.

"I think he likes you," Cheryl commented.

Tucker laughed and shook his head. "Sure he does." He pushed his own feelings away. Gerome fascinated him. There was a heart under all that stone, but Tucker wondered if he could ever truly reach it.

Cheryl bumped his arm. "I know when a man is interested, and he definitely is. The dark, stony types are the most passionate. Once you get through all that granite, there's usually an animal underneath." She was so bad sometimes, but Tucker still smiled. "Either that or more stone. It's a toss-up."

"Great," Tucker groused and went back to making breakfast.

"LET'S GO, Joshie," Cheryl said. "We have to go and see if I can get a job." She seemed even better now that she had eaten well. Tucker was ready, and he waited at the door for Joshie to put on his jacket. Then he locked the door and they left, taking the road toward the Driftwood.

It was a nice day, and Cheryl held Joshie's hand as he practically skipped along, singing and talking to himself. He seemed so happy to be outside, and Tucker had to agree with him. With Cheryl not feeling well, he had stayed close for the last few days, but now it seemed that the clouds might have blown away and the sun could come out. They both had a chance at jobs, and with those, maybe they could find someplace more permanent to live.

"I appreciate you taking care of me these last few days," Cheryl said above Joshie's excited chatter. "And watching him."

"Hey, it's no problem." Cheryl was like his sister, and he intended to hold on to the family he had. "You'd do the same for me." He looked both ways, and they crossed the street and the parking lot before going inside the bar, which was bright with the light flooding through the windows.

"Are you Cheryl?" the lady inside asked. "I'm Andi. Richard said you'd be coming in. We desperately need someone a few days a week." She seemed a little drawn, like she had been working too much and it was catching up with her. "Tucker?" she asked, and he nodded. "Knock on the door over there and ask for Richard or Alan. They'll want to talk to you."

Tucker left the others and followed her instructions, entering a small office.

"Tucker? I'm Richard. I believe you've met my friend Gerome and my husband, Daniel." They shook hands, and Richard motioned to the seat. "Gerome told me that you had some real kitchen skills."

"I started as a dishwasher and worked my way up to prep and did some cooking before my last job ended. What sort of help do you need?" He tried not to appear too excited, but his heart pounded. This was his chance at a job and maybe getting his life back on track. It was a real opportunity for him. "I cooked at home when I was a kid and can do just about anything you need." He felt himself beginning to stammer and stopped talking.

"Where did you work last?"

"The Wheelhouse in Tampa."

Richard whistled. "I know that restaurant, and I'm sorry you got caught up in that mess." It had been a big news story. The restaurant had been around for forty years, and the owner had passed away. The kids closed it and sold off the real estate. Tucker wasn't surprised Richard had heard about it. The restaurant was an institution, and when it was gone, Tucker had been out of a job.

"Yeah, me too."

"But that tells me you know enough to help us out here. I'm going to put you in touch with Zane, the chef in the kitchen, and you can meet him. He really needs someone to do prep and help him out."

"I'll do whatever you need me to." The knots that had taken up permanent residency in his belly unwound, and he finally thought that things might get better. "When do you want me to start?"

Richard chuckled. "Come in tomorrow and we'll get you all set. We're going to need your paperwork and Social Security card, stuff like that. Just bring it—we'll have you fill out the paperwork and go from there." He leaned forward. "I think you'll fit in well. We're only a small bar and restaurant…."

Tucker lowered his gaze. "What you are is saving my life," he said softly. He told himself he wasn't going to break down and took a deep breath to hold himself together. But he had been living on the edge for so long. Hunger, insecurity—all of it had haunted him, and he knew it was the same for Cheryl.

"What relationship is Cheryl to you?" Richard asked.

"She's like a sister. We met in one of the camps and have become close friends, and we need each other. We're like family, but not really related." He would do just about anything for her and Joshie. "When I met them, I was all alone and scared half out of my mind. Cheryl helped me get my feet back under me." He didn't know what would have happened to him if they hadn't met. "You guys doing this is…." He was at a loss for words.

Richard nodded. "We know what it's like to get a second chance."

Tucker hummed a second. "Gerome said something like that this morning. That there was someone who was important to him, and he was paying her back somehow."

"That would be Terrance's mother."

"The really big huge guy?" Tucker pursed his lips. "It's hard to think of him as having a mother. Though we all did, it's just that… dang, that guy is huge and…."

Richard chuckled. "She was something else, and we all try to live up to her in a way. I know this is difficult to understand fully, but Gerome has never done anything like this before. It's nice to see him taking an interest in someone."

"Is he why you're offering me this job?" Tucker asked.

Richard laughed outright. "Hell no. He said you have skills, and Zane will put you to the test to check just what they are. You're here because we need help and you know your way around a kitchen. It's that simple. Now it is true that Gerome brought those skills to my attention, but otherwise…." He shrugged.

"Good enough," Tucker said excitedly. "Is there anything else you'd like to know?"

Richard stood, and Tucker did the same. "We'll see you tomorrow, and I'll introduce you to Alan. He started the business and likes to get to know everyone."

They shook hands, and Tucker then left the office, almost unable to believe the good luck that had strung from a single, awful night.

He found Cheryl and Joshie in a booth, with a plate of french fries in front of Joshie. "Are you all done?" Cheryl asked. "Can you watch Joshie a minute? Andi said the boss wanted to see me."

"Of course," Tucker answered as he slipped into the booth. "Are those good?"

Joshie nodded, his cheeks stuffed like a hamster's. "Good."

"Take it easy. No one is going to take them away." Joshie swallowed twice before eating once again.

Some of the tables had filled for lunch, and Tucker was getting hungry himself. He snatched one of Joshie's fries and lifted one of the glasses of water from the table.

A couple entered and took a table in the center of the room, followed by another man Tucker recognized instantly. He walked stiffly, and his nose was swollen. Gerome had done a pretty good job of rearranging his face, but there was no mistaking the expensive clothes or the swagger in his walk. Tucker sank lower in the booth, turning to watch out the window. The inner door remained open, right behind the booth, and he hoped that partially obscured them. He hoped it would be enough and tried not to watch the guy, but it was difficult not to look every now and then. The guy stood at the bar, impatiently drumming his fingers on top of it.

Tucker once again turned away and forced himself not to pay attention to him, hoping the guy would just leave.

"Uh-oh…," Joshie said as water went all over the table.

"It's okay," Tucker said gently and grabbed some napkins to wipe up the spill. The last thing he wanted was anything to draw anyone's attention. The guy was still at the bar, but he leaned with his back against it, staring up at one of the televisions in the other corner. If he decided to watch the other television, he'd be staring right at Tucker and Joshie.

Tucker managed to sop up the water and gave Joshie some out of his glass, his heart pounding. Then he sank down into the booth, willing with everything he had for the guy to go away. And it seemed to be working until Gerome stepped inside.

Tucker saw the moment the guy recognized Gerome—and then him. The disinterested television-viewing gaze turned hard, the man's eyes filled with hatred, and his posture went from relaxed to rigid in a second. Gerome remained calm and strode over to the guy as though he owned the place.

Tucker couldn't hear what was said, but he saw the way both men went toe to toe. In a way it was exciting. Seeing Gerome take on someone that way and knowing he could protect himself was hot. Tucker had never thought that kind of power would be so exciting, but he was glad the table covered the evidence of just how turned on he was. He moved a little closer. "Go. Now. And stay away." Gerome's words reached Tucker's ears that time. "This is no place for the likes of you." Gerome pointed.

Tucker didn't hear the man's response, but he snatched a bag off the bar, tossed a few bills in that general direction, and strode slowly toward the door. Tucker was pretty sure he was posturing, the way his right hand twitched a little a dead giveaway.

"I didn't have a way to contact you," Tucker said when Gerome approached. He nodded, and Cheryl rejoined them, unaware of what had happened—and that was fine with Tucker.

"Did you spill?" Cheryl asked when she saw the glass filled with wet napkins.

"Tucker fixed it," Joshie said and ate the last of his fries. He looked a little like a tick, the way his full belly popped out.

"We should go," Cheryl said. "I'm feeling tired and I want to rest a little."

"I'll take you home. Let me get keys from Richard and I'll drive you." Gerome strode away.

Cheryl got Joshie wiped up and ready to go. Tucker paid the small bill for the fries, and they joined Gerome when he returned. Both he and Gerome seemed in agreement not to talk about what had happened in front of Cheryl.

The ride back to the apartment took just a few minutes, and then Cheryl went inside with Joshie.

"Let's go on down to the beach," Gerome suggested and pulled back out of the drive. He parked near the water and they got out to walk slowly up the nearly deserted beach.

"His name is Bobby Ramone. At least that's what he goes by." Gerome's expression was serious as they stayed just out of reach of the waves. "He's not a good man at all. At least based on what I could gather. He lives in Miami, apparently, and is someone we all need to stay away from."

"But you stared the guy down," Tucker said, more pleased by that than he thought he should be.

"Not much impresses me, and I needed to portray strength or he'd never have gone away," Gerome explained as he bent down to pick up a shell. He threw it into the water. "Guys like that only understand strength and intimidation. He's a bully at heart, like the mean kid on the playground." He threw another shell and then stopped, looking out to sea.

Tucker stood next to him, following Gerome's gaze to the shimmering water, the light catching the waves.

Neither of them moved, with only the lap of the waves and the cries of the seabirds breaking the still and quiet. Tucker's mind wandered for a few minutes before his attention settled on Gerome and the energy that seemed to radiate off him. Tucker looked to the side and found Gerome looking at him.

"Is something wrong?" He glanced downward to see if he might have had something on the front of his shirt. His T-shirt was old, but he hoped he hadn't spilled something on it.

"No," Gerome answered just above the breeze. "Everything is good."

"Then…," he began and swallowed hard as Gerome's gaze intensified, his brown eyes flecked with gold, growing even darker. In a second Tucker tried to remember anyone ever watching him as though they could see his soul. At first Tucker grew uncomfortable, but as he returned Gerome's gaze, he realized the man's walls were down and the hard edges on his expression had smoothed out. "Wow," he breathed.

"What?" Gerome asked.

"You look different. Less stressed and ready to punch someone." He smiled when Gerome did. "I like this look on you. It's nice." He turned back to the water.

"Not many people get to see it," Gerome said. "It's not a look I wear well."

"I don't think that's true. I think it's a look that you don't want others to see. There's a difference." Tucker shifted position slightly. "You must like the beach… or the company," he added hesitantly, and Gerome didn't contradict him. As Tucker watched a pod of dolphins frolicking offshore, Gerome touched his hand. It was fleeting and tentative, but then he did it again, and Tucker held a finger in return, just enough to tell Gerome that he noticed.

"My mom used to take me to the beach when I was a kid, and I used to love to build sand forts with moats and big defenses, stuff like that. We used to stay out for most of the day, as long as I was in the shade under this big umbrella. It was the centerpiece of many forts. She would read and rest while I played." He tried not to let the weight of loss settle over him. "This was a place I was happy."

"Me too. Different water, but the same kind of fun. I came with the guys, though, and we had the time of our lives. Terrance's mom would bring us. Looking back, I see it was a great way for three very active boys to run themselves out."

Tucker nodded. He figured his mom had done the same thing with him. "There were always other kids at the beach, and it was easy to make friends back then, even if it only lasted for the single day." How things had changed. "Now the only friend I really have is Cheryl." He turned to Gerome. "I guess I have a tendency to regard everyone else with suspicion. Maybe I should have done that the other day and just turned away. But I guess desperation makes for poor judgment."

"It can happen to anyone," Gerome replied and turned to him once more. Tucker met his gaze, and this time Gerome tugged him closer. He went along with the gentle pressure on his lower back, tilting his head as Gerome did the same.

Their kiss was surprisingly gentle, with Gerome holding back on the power Tucker felt banked behind him. His mind short-circuited and the waves and breeze all subsided, his full attention centered on exactly where Gerome's lips touched his. At that moment, nothing else mattered, as electricity shot up and down his spine in the most amazing way possible. Tucker wanted more; in fact, he wanted it all, everything. He'd have loved nothing more than to have Gerome take the kiss harder, and he pressed closer as a signal. Gerome tasted mildly of mint and heat, which only made Tucker want more. But Gerome pulled back, his gaze only adding to the warmth that suddenly surrounded Tucker like a bubble.

Tucker was speechless. He blinked, swallowed, and stared as Gerome watched him back. "O-kay…," he whispered. "I guess that answers all those questions." Tucker had been pretty sure Gerome was interested in him, but he didn't always read the signs correctly. This time it seemed he had gotten it right.

"Yeah, I guess it does," Gerome said in return.

Tucker nodded. "Is this something you do often? Kiss the boys, I mean?"

Gerome rolled his eyes. "Far less than I would like, but no. I am many things, some of which aren't so pretty, but I'm not a letch, and I don't go around luring guys into my lair."

Tucker groaned. "So you aren't the big bad wolf, even if you try to act that way sometimes." Maybe he was starting to get Gerome, just a little. He was honest, and yet partially hiding behind a thick wall of bravado, prickliness, and attitude. Tucker still hadn't figured out why Gerome felt the need for this, but knowing it was there was helpful.

"Yet sometimes I am as big a wolf as I appear." Now Gerome was just being enigmatic.

Tucker patted him on the shoulder. "If you say so." Two could play that bravado game, and Gerome actually pursed his lips as if wondering if Tucker was playing with him. He liked that he had set Gerome on his toes a little. Maybe it would make him more interesting. Tucker figured Gerome was the kind of man who liked being kept on his toes.

"We should get you back to the house," Gerome said.

Tucker shrugged. "Did you bring me down here so you could make a move on me?" A smile tickled the edges of his lips. "Not that I'm complaining in the least."

Gerome actually laughed. "No. I didn't know I was going to do that until it happened. I just intended to talk to you about our visitor today, but things got away from me."

"Okay. What do we do about this guy? It looks like he isn't going anywhere, and I think you can stare the guy down all you want, but he isn't going to just disappear." And as long as he was around, Tucker was going to have trouble with him. "I don't have whatever it is he thinks he can get from me."

A strange cloud passed across Gerome's expression. "I believe you." He looked out at the water once again. "And you aren't going to do anything. Just let me take care of it." The stony wall had snapped back into place, and Gerome seemed to draw away from him without ever taking a step. It was the strangest feeling.

"You aren't my boss or my father. I've been taking care of myself for a while, and I can continue to do it.

Just because you let me use the apartment doesn't mean that you own me." Tucker took a physical step away from Gerome. "I may not have much, but I have my own freedom, and—"

"I know you do," Gerome said firmly. "I wasn't insinuating anything else." He crossed his arms over his chest. "I know I'm a big guy, but I don't order people around or force them to do things they don't want to do."

Boy, had this conversation gone off the rails. Tucker wasn't quite sure how it had gone from gentle to harsh in a few seconds. "I never thought you did. All I meant is that Bobby Ramone is after *me*, and I can't let you do whatever it is you think you have to." He watched Gerome, his hands settling on his hips until Gerome faced him. "You know something that you aren't telling me. Maybe you have your own secrets, and that's fine. Just because you kissed me doesn't mean that I deserve to know what it is that you're holding on to so tightly. But if it has to do with me, then I have a right to know and to make my own decisions. I think you know what it feels like to have others deciding what's best for you."

Gerome's shoulders slumped slightly. "I do."

"Then at least let me make the decisions that affect me. Is that asking too much?" He wasn't going to back down with this. Gerome inhaled through his nose, and Tucker thought he was going to fight him. "You know he's going to be after you too."

"I can take care of myself," Gerome muttered and gave Tucker a stony look. Tucker recognized it from earlier at the bar.

Tucker stepped closer. He wasn't going to let Gerome intimidate him, even if that expression made him nervous. "So can I, Gerome. I've been doing it for a while." He stared right back at him. "What's our first step?"

Gerome didn't answer. "I don't know," he said, and Tucker snickered. He couldn't help it. The answer took him off guard. "I wasn't able to find out where he's staying or spends a lot of his time here."

"It has to be close. He stopped into the restaurant today for lunch, and it wasn't because he was looking for any of us. After he placed his order, he spent his time watching TV rather than watching the patrons. He felt safe there. I think he was surprised when you came in, and then he saw me. I was trying to stay out of his line of sight."

Gerome nodded. "I'll ask Richard if he's seen him around. Maybe he is a local, but I doubt it. His clothes are way too expensive for anything bought around here."

Tucker figured that was true. "I can't help you there."

"Come on. I need to get you to the apartment, and I need to get back to work."

"That was a pretty long lunch break," Tucker observed.

"The boss was in the store today and she gave me a couple of hours because of all I worked over the holidays. But I should get back."

Tucker hoped Gerome would take this private time to kiss him again, but instead he turned back toward the car.

"Gerome," Tucker said.

Gerome paused and looked back. Tucker caught his gaze, holding it as he drew nearer. This time he initiated the kiss, holding Gerome, pressing hard, taking what he wanted.

The frisson of energy he'd felt during their earlier kiss returned with a vengeance, and Gerome wound his arms around him, sliding a hand into his hair. This time Gerome didn't hold back, crushing him close enough that Tucker felt Gerome's excitement hard and firm between them. Holy hell, the man was big everywhere. Tucker kept his eyes closed, his mind on everything that was happening between them. Each firm touch added to the excitement, and Tucker wanted to feel Gerome's hands everywhere. They stayed on his back, though, holding him in place, which was perfect. Tucker didn't want to go anywhere.

He used his lips to tug on Gerome's, earning him a soft moan. He smiled, sliding his eyes open to gaze into Gerome's. "You liked that." They were both shaking, and Tucker realized he was the cause. It was heady to think he could make the big man react that way. Gerome seemed to be about control, so having him lose it over a kiss was intensely hot.

"We do need to go," Tucker whispered hoarsely. "Though I'd love to let you maul me some more." His smirk was precious, and he followed Gerome off the beach and back to the car. When he got in and settled, Gerome squeezed his hand before starting the engine.

Chapter 5

"I'M NOT sure what this guy is up to, but I'd certainly like to find out," Gerome told Richard once the store was closed and he had a few minutes to meet with him in the office at the restaurant. Alan, now Richard's business partner, was tending the bar for a little while. "Have you seen him in here before?"

"Yes. A few times over the past month," Richard answered. "Not before that. If he's living here, then he just relocated. You followed him from the bar that night to the camp where you found Tucker. Did he stop anywhere?"

"No." It was frustrating. "It was a fucking daisy chain that night. We were both following Tucker, at least to start, but I ended up following him following

Tucker. He stayed on him like glue, not that it was hard to do. Tucker just walked home."

"Then I suggest you pick up his trail somewhere and find out what he's up to. My suggestion might be to start at one of the marinas. If he's doing business by boat, then he might be staying there or hanging around."

Gerome nodded, wishing he had thought of that. It was such an obvious answer. "Tucker wants to help," he said. "He's got some fire in him."

Richard leaned back in his squeaky chair and laughed. "Of course he does. You wouldn't be this twisted up over a guy who didn't."

Gerome wanted to growl, but he kept his reaction to himself. "I'm just helping the guy."

Richard snorted. "Don't bullshit me. I can see the light in your eyes from all the way over here. You smile every time you mention his name."

"So you're saying that I'm acting the same way you do around Daniel?" he countered.

"Yeah. What's wrong with that?" Richard glanced at the door. "Our lives before Longboat Key are gone, over and done. We can't go back, no matter how much we bitch and moan about it. There's nothing wrong with being happy and finding someone who makes you want to fucking live again rather than just exist."

"Terrance—"

"What about him?" Richard countered before Gerome could finish his thought. "He's just as lost as we all were. The thing is, I found my way out, and you're starting to do the same. Terrance is having a harder time of it."

Gerome sat back. "You know we sound like a bunch of gossipy grandmothers having tea and talking about their grandchildren." He stretched out his legs. "Maybe you should put a couch in here so we can all take turns talking about our feelings." He rolled his eyes.

Richard scowled. "Just get out, and be careful. This guy knows what both of you look like."

That was something Gerome knew he was going to need to change.

"YOU WANTED to help," Gerome told Tucker the following day as they changed clothes.

They had both finished work at four. Now Gerome handed Tucker a baseball cap and sunglasses. Daniel had already shortened Tucker's hair. He was dressed in jeans and a flannel shirt. Gerome had a cooler and a tackle box.

"But is this going to be enough?" Tucker asked.

"Sure it is. The day is sunny, and you look different enough with the haircut and hat. Ramone has seen you a few times, but this is just different enough, and he isn't going to be watching for you. Just the opposite—we're looking for him."

Gerome looked him over. Tucker looked really good in those tight, slightly threadbare jeans. Thoughts of the kiss on the beach rushed over him. Still, they had a task to do, and he didn't need to get himself worked up. "All we're going to do is check out some of the marinas looking like fishermen. There are some we can't get into because they're private and gated, but others are open, and I thought we would start with those."

"Can I go too?" Joshie asked. "I wanna catch fish."

Gerome knelt down. "Not today, buddy. But I promise that we'll all go fishing soon so you can catch something. Is that okay?" Joshie nodded. "Maybe we can go see the manatees on my next day off. Would you like that?"

"Manatees," he agreed, racing across the room, bounding onto the sofa.

"We'll be back in a few hours," Gerome told Cheryl, who once again seemed a little pale.

"You two have fun with your skulking," she teased as she finished the dishes. "Joshie and I are going to watch a little TV. I'm supposed to start work tomorrow, and I want to be rested." She wiped her hands and joined Joshie in the living room. "It's been a while."

"I'm off, so I'll be here with him," Tucker reassured her, and then he and Gerome left the apartment and piled into the truck.

"Let's try the one nearest the Driftwood. If Ramone has been coming there, then he might be staying nearby." At least that seemed logical. Gerome pulled into the nearly full parking area, and they got out. He grabbed the cooler and handed Tucker the tackle box.

"It's empty," Tucker observed.

"These are props, nothing more. Just keep your head, and if you see him, say something quietly but don't draw any attention. When we're out on the dock, act like you know where you're going and you belong there. We've chartered one of the boats for the evening, if anyone asks. Its name is *Jeff's Joy*. It doesn't exist, so no one will have heard of it, but it will be enough for a good cover." Gerome closed the cooler cover and motioned Tucker forward. "Just relax. You look like you're marching into battle rather than looking forward to a few hours on the water."

"I'll try," Tucker said, stopping. "Maybe this wasn't such a good idea." He turned his gaze back toward the car. "How do you know about this stuff, anyway?"

Gerome shrugged. "Television." It was the quickest answer and seemed to suffice. "Just relax and take it easy. Keep aware of what's going on around you. Just listen to the sound of the water and the birds. You belong here and just want to have a good time. You'll be fine."

Tucker relaxed his stance, and they entered the dock area. It wasn't very big, so they headed first in one direction and then the other. "What boat are we looking for again?" Tucker asked.

"*Jeff's Joy*," Gerome answered as they watched both sides of the dock.

"I don't think it's here. Maybe we have the wrong place?" he said, and Gerome flashed him a smile.

"I guess maybe we do. I thought this was the one, but I might have had my directions mixed up." Gerome motioned back the way they came, pleased that Tucker was playing along. There were a few people out on the decks of their boats, and if they overheard anything, it would be the two of them sounding confused.

"Is that it over there?" Tucker asked as he stopped. He didn't point, but Gerome followed his gaze. Sure enough, the guy looked like Ramone, but Tucker shook his head as the guy drew closer and turned. "I guess not."

They went back to the car and loaded their stuff. Tucker got in, shaking in his seat. "That was so much fun. It was like we were spies or something. I guess I expected more people to be out."

"I don't know about spies, but the rest…." Gerome pulled out, and they moved on to the next marina, and the following one. The sun was beginning to set as they approached the last marina for the night.

"It's going to get dark," Tucker said softly before they got out of the truck.

"We'll make a quick pass and then get out of here before we can't see anything." They decided to leave their cover props behind and hurried out toward the dock area.

"I can't really see much," Tucker whispered, their footsteps echoing on the wooden planking.

Gerome took his hand as they checked out the area. He wasn't sure what he expected to find. The boats were mostly dark, and there was no one around. They went down to the few with lights, but Ramone definitely wasn't on either of them, though the soft cries that emanated from one clearly indicated that *someone* was there and very pleased with whatever God was providing.

"Let's get out of here," Gerome said. Why he had thought this might be fruitful was beyond him. He should have known they weren't likely to find this guy like this.

"Is that him?" Tucker asked as they turned the corner, just up from the entrance.

Gerome stopped and nodded. Taking a step back into the shadow of one of the boats, he hoped all to hell that Ramone would turn the other way. But he didn't. Gerome tugged Tucker to him and did a James Bond, kissing him right there, folding his body close. Damn, Tucker was hot enough to nearly pull his attention away from where he needed it. Ramone paused a second at the junction, saw them, and quickly headed away without looking back.

Tucker pulled away. "Is he gone?" he asked, and Gerome nodded. "Are you going to kiss me some more or follow him?"

"We don't need to follow. I know where he is." Gerome motioned Tucker around. One of the boats that had been dark was now lighted. "Go back to the truck." He pressed his keys into Tucker's hand. "Get in, stay down, and lock the doors. I'll be right there."

Gerome headed down the dock, and Tucker thankfully took off. Once it was quiet again, Gerome continued down to the boat, making a note of the name, *Sweet Paradise*. Then he quietly backed away and hurried to the truck. He knocked on the window and Tucker let him inside.

He started the engine, and they took off. "That was scary," Tucker said.

"Maybe a little. But I know the boat name." He figured he could watch the boat and pay a visit when Bobby Ramone was off somewhere else just to see what the guy was up to.

"I have to ask—do you do this sort of thing a lot? You sure seem to know what you're doing." Tucker buckled himself in as Gerome got them out of there. "Are you sure you aren't a police officer or something?" He inhaled sharply. "Are you a spy?"

Gerome chuckled. "No. I'm neither one."

"A criminal mastermind after whatever business this guy is doing?" That was a little too close to home. "I know I'm being stupid."

Gerome pulled off the side of the road. "This man has come after you, and he isn't going to stop. If he's involved in anything criminal, and that seems likely to me, then he can't have you around to talk to anyone. He needs to stay under the radar, and you're a threat to that. We know where he stays, and we know the boat that this bundle that he wanted you to pick up might have fallen off of. Now we need to figure out what that stuff was. Once we do, we can let the police handle it all." Then he could stay out of it.

If Gerome were honest, though, he liked the action. It felt something like what he'd done in Detroit, and it got his blood pumping and gave him back a sense of purpose.

"I suppose you're going to go back and see what's going on. Like break into the boat." Tucker's gaze was deadly serious. "Not that I'm going to stop you, but you aren't going alone."

"Are you intending to come? You were nervous the entire time."

Tucker sat straighter in the seat. "Of course I'm going to come with you. Someone has to be the lookout in case the guy comes back. You don't want to get caught, do you?" He smiled in the darkness. "You didn't leave me hanging out to dry when Bobby Ramone came gunning for me in the tent camp, and I'm not going to leave you hanging now."

Tucker leaned closer, and Gerome did the same. Their lips met in a gentle kiss. Gerome tipped forward a little too much, and they ended up laughing as Tucker lightly bonked his head. Gerome sat back up and checked the rearview mirror before pulling back onto the road.

He found himself surprisingly happy, and the short drive wasn't nearly long enough. Gerome parked and sat back in the seat with the engine off. He was tempted to ask Tucker to come in with him, but he didn't quite know how. Usually, if he liked a guy, Gerome went for it. They would have some fun for a few hours or a couple of days, then part company. It was easy to ask for that kind of fling. Make eye contact, talk, flirt, and then just ask. He was handsome and powerful, he knew that, and most of the time he got an affirmative.

That wasn't the kind of thing he was looking for with Tucker, and quite frankly he didn't know what his next move should be. He'd been the one to initiate their first kiss, but Tucker hadn't been shy after that. Gerome had been hoping for some sort of indication from Tucker about what he wanted, but so far it had only been kisses that left Gerome breathless.

Tucker hadn't moved either, and Gerome wondered what he was thinking. Maybe he was just waiting for an invitation, though Tucker didn't seem shy about what he wanted.

God, this was confusing. Gerome wanted to do this right. He opened the door and climbed out without saying a word, his thoughts swirling. Glancing over the top of the truck, he waited for Tucker and then walked him inside to his door. "I should probably say good night." His head spun, and part of him wanted to just go inside so he could try to figure some shit out. That was what he did. Back in Detroit, Richard was the manager, the guy in charge, Terrance was the muscle, and Gerome was the idea man. It was his promotions, hype, and forward thinking that helped get them where they were.

"I should make sure that Cheryl and Joshie are okay," Tucker whispered.

Gerome nodded. That message was clear enough for him. Tucker drew closer and stood on his toes to kiss him before opening the door and going inside.

Gerome's apartment was dark, but he could see it was still furnished with the drab items the government provided. He hadn't bothered to change much, especially not out in the main room. The chairs and sofa were beige, and the carpet was gray. Gerome hadn't put up any pictures of his own, so only bland, abstract pieces that engendered little interest hung on the walls. The apartment didn't feel like home, and it never really would. It was a place to live, a roof over his head and little more.

Gerome tossed his keys on the counter and pulled open the refrigerator door. He hadn't eaten dinner and figured he could make a sandwich before relaxing in front of something inane on television. He needed a distraction to take his thoughts off Tucker, who seemed to consume them.

He'd just settled on the sofa with a beer and his sandwich and had turned on the television when someone knocked on his door. Gerome checked his phone and grabbed a beer on his way to the door, figuring it was Terrance. "Hey, I was wondering if you'd—" He paused when he saw that Tucker was standing on the mat. "Hey…," he said softly, peering across at the closed apartment door. "Is everything okay?" He set the beer on the counter.

Tucker nodded. "Cheryl is getting Joshie ready for bed, and then she's going to go to bed, and…." He leaped.

Gerome hesitated a fraction of a second before catching Tucker in his arms. Tucker wrapped his legs around Gerome's waist, and damned if Gerome didn't find his hands filled with the globes of Tucker's butt.

He kissed hard, and Gerome nearly lost his balance before backing slowly inside. Tucker pushed the door closed and resumed plundering his mouth. Heat rolled off Tucker, and Gerome's body reacted instantly. His pants were too damned tight, and his cock ached just having Tucker in his arms. "Are you sure about this?" Gerome had to ask. Before he probably would have taken without thinking, but this was Tucker, and he needed to know that this was truly what Tucker wanted.

"God, yes!" Tucker groaned as Gerome massaged his butt and made his way to the bedroom, the food on the coffee table forgotten in the excitement of the feast right in front of him.

The one extravagance that Gerome had allowed himself was his bedding. It was rich, royal blue, thick, soft, and plush. He laid Tucker on the bed, the duvet puffing around him as if it, too, wanted to touch Tucker.

"Wow, this is nice," Tucker breathed, still holding him around the neck. Gerome ran his hands under Tucker's shirt, pushing the fabric upward, exposing his lightly dusted belly to Gerome's hungry gaze. He leaned forward, burying his nose against Tucker's skin, inhaling the rich, musky, masculine scent of him, letting it work its magic in the excited recesses of his mind, stoking fires that already blazed hot.

He ran his hand over Tucker's firm yet soft belly, teasing his way upward, taking the fabric right along. A pink nipple slipped from under the shirt, and he flicked it with his tongue. Tucker moaned softly, so he did it again, teasing the bud with his tongue until it was firm.

Gerome worked Tucker's shirt off, basking in the glow of beautiful honey-warm skin. God, Tucker was stunning. Gerome had been imagining what Tucker looked like without his clothes on for days. He'd gotten tantalizing glimpses, but this was a feast of masculine beauty. And Gerome was willing to bet Tucker had no idea how gorgeous he was.

"What are you doing?" Tucker asked, folding his arms over his chest. "Is something wrong?"

"God, no," he breathed softly. "Everything is perfect."

And it was. Gerome closed his eyes and realized that the perfect man, the one of his dreams, the guy that he conjured up in his fantasies, was lying in front of him. Not that he had fantasized about Tucker specifically, but a man like him, with those deep blue eyes flecked with green, and soft, luminous hair.

Tucker smiled and let his arms fall to his sides, giving Gerome a view of all of him. Gerome tugged his shirt out of his pants and pulled it off, baring himself to Tucker, who reached up, his fingertips glancing over Gerome's chest and belly. He leaned closer, and Tucker sat up, his hands roaming and discovering. Gerome closed his eyes, taking in the sensation of first exploration.

He drew Tucker down and kissed him, their chests pressing together. Gerome loved the feel of Tucker against him, wrapping him in his arms and pressing them together as he devoured Tucker's lips.

Tucker arched under him, and Gerome took the chance to open his pants and slip them down. He wanted more, and Tucker held his hips up so Gerome could finish undressing him.

Naked, Tucker was even more stunning. Gerome slipped off the bed, shucking his shoes and slipping out of his jeans and the rest of his clothes before climbing back onto the bed. He wanted Tucker more than he had desired anyone in his life, and that was a little fearsome. Gerome knew he could fall for Tucker. He was fearful sometimes but did what was needed anyway. And Tucker wasn't afraid to take what he wanted, even from Gerome, which was saying something.

Tucker pulled him down, enveloping Gerome in his arms and legs, wrapping around him tightly. "I want to touch everything and get to know all of you at once."

He chuckled slightly. "And there's a lot of you to get to know." Tucker patted his butt and then grabbed hold. "I've never been with a guy as strong and powerful as you. It's like you could break me if you wanted, but you never would." Tucker sucked at the base of his neck.

"Of course not," Gerome nearly whined, stretching his neck at the intensity of sensation. "This isn't about power."

Tucker pulled away, his gaze boring into Gerome's. "I know that sometimes it is. Sex and relationships can sometimes be about nothing but power." He patted Gerome's chest. "You could be that way if you wanted, but I don't sense that at all."

Gerome smiled. Yeah, sometimes sex had been about power and expressing who was in charge. Gerome had experienced a battle of wills in the bedroom on a few occasions, and he hadn't really enjoyed it. "To me, being with someone is about mutual pleasure and happiness. That's when it's at its best." He kissed Tucker again before sliding his tongue down Tucker's chin and along his throat. He caressed his sides and belly, moving down to his hips and quivering thighs. Damn, he loved that reaction. It made him feel as though he were important, and Gerome hadn't felt that way since Detroit. Maybe he did like the fact that he had power… but this time power meant the ability to make Tucker feel good and make those deep, throaty moans he would never tire of hearing. "What is it you like?"

Tucker lifted his head as though he didn't understand or had simply never been asked the question.

"Didn't the people you were with before ever ask?" Tucker shrugged, and Gerome narrowed his eyes. "Didn't they take the time to make it special?"

Tucker groaned softly. "Not everyone cares." He sighed, and Gerome took Tucker's hands in his.

"Well, I do." Then he smiled. "And I get to try to figure it out." He sucked at one of Tucker's nipples, already knowing that he enjoyed it. "How about…?" He licked his way down Tucker's fluttering belly and then over to the top of his hip, sucking lightly at the soft spot just above the bone. He knew if he got the pressure right, the sensation would be somewhere between a tickle and a tease, and… that was it. Tucker gasped and groaned deeply. Perfection. "Maybe this…?" He shifted lower, spreading Tucker's legs, trailing his fingers, followed by his lips, up Tucker's inner thighs, until he slid his lips along Tucker's length.

Tucker stilled, not even taking a breath, as though he expected Gerome to pull back at any moment. "Please…," Tucker whispered under his breath, so softly Gerome wasn't even sure the word was really there. And yet it was, and he slipped his lips over the head and down his length, drawing Tucker deliciously across his tongue.

Tucker quivered and gasped. It was a glorious sound that grew deeper and more guttural as Gerome went down. "Gerome…." His name hung in the air.

"Say it again," he whispered after pulling away. "Say my name again." It made him breathless just to hear it, and when Tucker repeated himself, Gerome was determined to take Tucker all the way to heaven.

"Gerome…," Tucker whispered.

Gerome heard it like a prayer of ecstasy and did his very best to deliver.

He desperately wanted inside Tucker's hot body. His cock throbbed at the very idea skirting through his head. But Gerome wasn't sure Tucker was ready for that. Some guys fucked after exchanging names and saying hello. If he were truthful, Gerome had been one of those guys. All he'd needed was a willing partner and a condom and he was ready to go. It would be so easy to fall back into those old patterns with Tucker, but he couldn't allow it. Gerome admitted to himself, with Tucker's scent all around him and his taste fresh on his tongue, that he wanted something more. And a different result required a different approach.

Tucker's cock throbbed, and Gerome deduced that he was close. His eyes were wide as saucers, a light sheen of sweat made Tucker's skin glisten, and damned if Tucker's entire body didn't vibrate under him. "Don't stop…," Tucker hummed almost to himself as a sort of mantra.

Gerome had no intention of pausing. He took Tucker harder, and Tucker outright shook, his gorgeous eyes clamping shut as his release came over him, and Gerome tasted Tucker as he burst on his tongue.

Gerome swallowed and stilled when Tucker did, letting the postrelease headiness float through Tucker. It was the best feeling Gerome knew, though it lasted just a few seconds before Tucker's eyes slid open, his lips curling upward. "Were you trying to kill me?"

"I don't think it's really possible to suck a guy's brains out through his dick," Gerome teased with a grin as he licked his lips to get the last of Tucker's essence.

"Well…." Tucker sat up and pushed Gerome back down onto the bedding. Gerome ended up with his head at the foot of the bed and Tucker on top of him. "Maybe it's my turn to try."

Gerome had not expected this. He had never experienced playfulness in bed, and damned if it didn't add to the excitement. Tucker seemed to smile constantly, and the wicked gleam in his eyes told Gerome that he was in for quite a ride.

And it seemed he was right. Tucker returned the passion and pleasure in equal measure, driving Gerome out of his mind until his head throbbed and his eyes crossed. “Tucker… honey, I don’t think the challenge was meant to be taken literally,” Gerome muttered and let his head fall back as Tucker sucked him deep and hard, using his lips and fingers to produce a symphony of excitement that Gerome was powerless to control.

Tucker had him transfixed, pulling his gaze to where he sank between those sweet lips. The sight was almost more than he could bear, let alone the intense heat and pressure that accompanied the visual. He groaned and whimpered, a steady stream of nonsense filling his head and slipping out between his own lips. And all he could do was lie still and let it happen. Every time he moved, Tucker placed his hand flat on his belly to hold him in place. What shocked him most was that this was about giving, rather than taking. He almost didn’t know what to make of it.

He felt like an inexperienced teenager with the way that Tucker seemed to understand him, taking Gerome to the edge and backing away before doing it again. God, it was as though Tucker knew exactly what Gerome liked. It was uncanny and strikingly erotic at the same time.

“Tucker….” His tone sounded like a warning to his own ears, even as he gripped the bedding. Tucker had complete control, and he seemed to like it. His eyes shone when he glanced up, and Gerome sweated as heat built around him. He inhaled deeply, afraid to look away from Tucker in case all of this was a dream.

Tucker pulled away, and Gerome clamped his eyes closed, stifling the groan that threatened to escape. He missed the heat and wetness, but mostly Tucker. He blinked and brought Tucker's lips to his. "Is everything all right?"

Tucker nodded. "I just didn't want things to be over."

Gerome chuckled. "I see." He had been so close to the edge for long enough that his entire body vibrated with built-up energy. He was seconds from rolling Tucker on the bed, ready to take him here and now. Instinct kicked in and his control waned quickly, but he held himself back. Fortunately, Tucker seemed to understand and took him once again, driving Gerome to the brink of passion and then over the edge, both of them groaning as Gerome flew into his release.

Slowly the spinning room settled, and he came back to himself to find Tucker right next to him, an arm over his belly, snuggled in close, warmth surrounding him. Gerome rolled onto his side, pulling Tucker against him. Their kiss was soft, languid, like it could go on for days. The heat of passion and excitement was spent, and now Gerome was content with quiet.

He had to wonder what the hell had happened to him. Gerome lay with his eyes closed, happy. He'd always had a million things to do and had to go and move all the time. His life had been high-energy, and now he was happy to simply be still. Something had changed, and Gerome wasn't sure if it was good or not. Having Tucker right next to him was amazing; that wasn't the issue at all. It was inside. Something in him had shifted, and Gerome wondered when the hell that had happened. He sighed softly, not moving, as his thoughts raced in circles. His body was still, but his head refused to be—especially at the notion that he didn't *want* to move, that he was truly content.

"Why does life seem temporary?"

"What?" Tucker asked, and Gerome realized he had spoken out loud.

"Sorry…," Gerome said without moving.

"No. You're right. It is temporary. Home, security, family, all of it is temporary." Tucker rolled over and shifted a little away. "Everything can be very temporary. And that's the scariest thing of all. We can take a lot of things for granted, and then they're gone." He sighed and rested his head on Gerome's arm. "Sorry. I didn't mean to get so maudlin."

"No need. I guess…. There's been a lot of change in my life too, and I was just feeling sorry for myself." He had been having a months-long pity party because he was here and not back in Detroit, when in truth he and the guys had made their choice, and their lives here were the result of that. This wasn't anyone's doing but their own. Gerome slipped closer to Tucker and closed his eyes. "You know, I never did get any dinner. It seemed that I was going to eat, and a certain neighbor came by with dessert that was too good to pass up."

"I see. And who is this neighbor, and do I need to be threatened by these tasty treats? Or should I scratch his eyes out?" Tucker chuckled.

Gerome pulled him closer. "You're a goof," he whispered and kissed Tucker's words away. "Come on, let's eat before I waste away to nothing." He got up, pulled on a light robe, and tossed an older one to Tucker.

GEROME WOKE the following morning to a new sensation. He wasn't alone, and Tucker had snuggled right up next to him. He didn't want to move, but he rolled over, checking the time on the clock on the nightstand. "Tucker…." He breathed softly. "I think we need to get up."

A grumble followed, and Tucker burrowed deeper under the covers. "It's too early."

"I need to get into work, and so will Cheryl," Gerome said, pushing away the covers. "Come on."

"I was never a morning person," Tucker admitted. "As a kid I used to love to sleep until noon and stay out really late. Lately I go to bed when the sun sets because it's just easier than fighting for light and batteries." He sat up and leaned on Gerome's shoulders. "I'm so grateful to you for what you've done for me… for us." He didn't move.

An idea hit Gerome like a two-by-four. "Is that why you came last night?"

Tucker gasped. "No. I don't pay my debts with my body. How can you ask that?"

"Then what are you getting at?" Gerome pulled away, wondering what he had been missing.

"Nothing. I was just saying thank you." Tucker stared at him. "Why would you think there would be anything else?"

"Because everyone wants something," Gerome said.

Tucker glared at him and then smacked him on the shoulder.

"What?"

"Sometimes you are such an ass," Tucker said with a smile. "I said the same thing about you, and now you can't accept that I would be nice to you without wanting something in return." Tucker climbed out of the bed and began gathering his clothes.

Gerome hesitated, trying to discern whether Tucker was angry. Normally he wouldn't care. He found himself watching his body language and his lips, but they were no help.

"Do you want breakfast?" Gerome asked.

"It's late, and you're right. I need to check on Cheryl to make sure she's ready for work. I'm watching Joshie today, and there will be things that she's going to need." He pulled on his pants and tugged his shirt over his head.

Gerome climbed out of the bed, not bothering with his clothes, and stopped Tucker by hugging him tightly. He didn't apologize, because he wasn't sure if he should, if he needed to, if Tucker wanted him to. Dammit, he felt like a fucking teenager on a first date, and it sucked big-time. Tucker turned in his embrace. "Stop by after you're done with work if you like."

"I will," Tucker promised and kissed him. Hopefully Gerome had his answer. "I'll see you later." He patted Gerome's butt as he stepped away. "Damn, are you made of rocks?"

Gerome chuckled and struck a pose, flexing his arms and shoulders. He did it to be funny, but Tucker stared a second and licked his lips. Then he left the room, and Gerome shook his head, making his way to the bathroom to start his day.

"GEROME!" TUCKER called just as Gerome stepped out of the shower. He grabbed a towel and raced, dripping, into the living room.

"What is it? What's wrong?" He was ready for action, even in only a towel.

"Bobby Ramone is out in front. I saw him on the sidewalk." Tucker went to the window, and Gerome pulled him back. He peered outside but didn't see anyone.

"He isn't there now." Gerome wasn't sure what to say. "You stay inside with the doors locked and call me right away if you see or hear anything. Don't open the door for anyone, and I'll check things out on my way to work."

He didn't like this at all. It made sense that Bobby would continue to hunt Tucker down. Losing that brick of money was going to drive him crazy. It was stupid of him to have asked Tucker to try to retrieve it, and Tucker should have turned away from the offer, but it had been too tempting. Gerome understood that.

"Okay. Will you see that Cheryl gets to work okay?"

Gerome nodded. "I need to leave in half an hour. I can drive her in."

"Thank you," Tucker said softly. "Ummm…." He swallowed and his eyes widened. "You're practically naked." His cheeks grew red. "There isn't enough time, though…."

"Not that you didn't see everything last night," Gerome teased. "I should go get dressed."

"You don't have to. If you went into work like that, the ladies would be beating a path to your door."

Gerome chuckled as he left the room. "And so would the police. Somehow I don't think wearing a towel is appropriate outdoor dress." Still, he was fully aware of Tucker. He left the room before he could rip off the towel and show Tucker just how much he liked the idea of staying here with him.

Dressing didn't take long, and he walked Tucker back across the hall. He made sure Cheryl was ready and left with her.

Gerome watched carefully as they turned out of the parking lot, but he didn't see anyone hanging around. He hoped Tucker's imagination wasn't running away with him.

"Are you ready for this?" Gerome asked.

Cheryl nodded, her leg bouncing. "It's been a while. It will be nice to make some money again. I hope I look okay. Richard didn't say what I should wear, and I tried for something similar to the way Andi was dressed, but I don't have very much, and… well, it's clean. I guess that's the most important thing." She was clearly really nervous.

"Richard is a good boss who will look out for you. There's really nothing for you to be nervous about. The lunch crowd is pretty easygoing, and everyone is friendly."

Cheryl sighed. "Tucker asked me to keep an eye out for the guy who came after him." She bit her lower lip. "I'm wondering what he got himself into. When he told me about what he was being offered, I tried to talk him out of it, but it was a lot of money. I wanted him to be careful."

"He didn't find anything, though I doubt this guy believes him," Gerome explained. "How are you feeling?"

Cheryl sighed. "Honestly, I'm tired. Really tired a lot of the time. I've been on the edge for a long time. It's hard to worry where I'm going to get the food so Joshie can eat, let alone make sure he has clothes and shoes." She turned, looking out the window a minute before Gerome pulled into the restaurant parking lot.

"The door should be open. Just go on in and Richard and Andi will take care of getting you started."

Cheryl nodded. "Thanks for taking a chance on us. I know it takes a lot of… whatever you got that you saw to make you help us. It took guts and maybe even a touch of faith. I'll do my best to not let you down."

Gerome shook his head. "Don't let yourself down. That's all that matters." Where the hell that came from, Gerome wasn't sure. But it sounded right, and he wanted her to be just a little more confident. "Just do your best and give it your all…. Think of Joshie." Go him being motivational. "Put on your best smile and dazzle those customers." He waited for her to get out and smiled all the way to work.

Chapter 6

"MOMMY," JOSHIE cried as soon as Cheryl walked in the door from work. She was all smiles and hugs but seemed drawn around her eyes.

"Are you feeling all right?" Tucker asked.

"Just tired. It was a lot of activity. But I'll get used to it." She released Joshie from the hug. "Go on and play, sweetheart." She stood, watching as Joshie returned to his trucks, running them over the floor. He certainly loved them. "Everyone there was really nice."

"They're good people." Tucker sat on the sofa. "How did you get home?"

"I walked. It wasn't that far. I started the car before coming in to make sure it doesn't crap out on us if we need it. Maybe when I get paid, I can have it properly licensed and things. It would be good to be able to go places."

Tucker nodded but somehow didn't think that was the best way to use some of the first money they received.

Cheryl emptied her pockets and placed over seventy dollars on the counter.

"I'd say people liked you," Tucker said, smiling at the small pile of money.

"It was busy, and there were only two of us. It came back to me pretty quickly. Don't make unnecessary trips and always have your hands full going to or from the kitchen." She smiled and lowered herself into the chair, leaning back and closing her eyes.

"I'll make some dinner pretty soon if you want to lie down," Tucker offered as a knock sounded. He answered it to find Gerome outside. "What's up?" He smiled, his cheeks heating as he remembered the night before.

Gerome leaned down to kiss him. "I think you and I need to go visiting," he explained softly. "I went by on the way home, and it seems very quiet. It might be a good time to try to look around."

"I see." Tucker's heart beat faster, and he grew heated with excitement. He nodded. "I'll meet you at your place in ten?"

Gerome agreed, and Tucker closed the door before changing into the hat and getting the sunglasses he'd used before. After explaining that he wouldn't be too long, he said goodbye to Joshie and Cheryl and joined Gerome at his place.

Gerome greeted him shirtless at the door, and Tucker basked in the heat that flowed through him. Damn, this man was fine in all the right ways. He wondered if he could talk Gerome out of this little escapade and just head for the bedroom. He closed the distance between them and wrapped his arms around Gerome's neck, diving right into the kiss. Gerome let him take control, giving and exploring Tucker's mouth, holding him closer, his heat penetrating Tucker's shirt. Tucker's excitement grew just being near him, and he rested his head on Gerome's shoulder, standing still and enjoying the moment.

"We really should go," Gerome whispered, but neither of them moved. Gerome must have been as comfortable as he was. It was nice just being held for a while. Tenderness hadn't been part of his life in quite some time. "I should get dressed so we can find out what's going on."

Tucker sighed. "You know, I'm really starting to hate this guy. He seems to show up at the most inopportune times." He pulled away and waited while Gerome finished dressing… which was a pity. Gerome could cause quite a distraction if he simply walked up and down the dock.

"I'm ready," Gerome said, and they made the quick drive to the marina. Tucker put on the hat and sunglasses and pulled out the tackle box.

"Take this," Gerome told him. "I borrowed it from Terrance. It's his old phone, and he didn't stop service on it." He unlocked it and showed Tucker the code. "All you need to do is text me if you see anyone coming toward the boat or if Ramone makes an appearance. Then grab your stuff and head back to the car. Don't draw attention to yourself by running; just bury your attention in the phone and no one is going to pay any attention to you. People on their phones are annoying as all hell to the rest of the world, so most of the time you'll get ignored and they'll be glad you're gone."

"What if he recognizes me?" Tucker asked.

"Push him into the water and take off. He isn't going to be expecting any sort of attack, so make one and then run." That was easy advice for Gerome to give—he was strong. Tucker wasn't built that way. Gerome got out of the truck. "Use your weight to unbalance him. He'll fall before he can recover."

"Okay. I'll try." Tucker closed the door and took the gear, following Gerome out onto the dock. He went as far as the intersection three boats down from the one Gerome pointed out. He set down the box, leaned against the piling, and pulled out the phone. Like Gerome said, he pretended to be looking something up and glanced around to make sure no one was coming.

He saw no one, but his heart pounded hard enough he could almost hear it. Gerome was nowhere to be seen. Tucker continued with the charade.

A group of ladies approached down the dock. "Can we help you?" one of them asked. Tucker had hoped they would just pass by. "This is a private dock."

"I'm sorry," Tucker said softly. "A friend said that he was going to meet me here so we could go out, but he isn't answering his phone or texts. He may be in the car and can't answer." He did his best to look confused and hoped he didn't come across like he needed to pee or something. "I'll give him a few more minutes and then give up, I guess."

The women nodded and continued down the way.

Tucker sent Gerome a text that they were approaching. The women boarded a sleek, fancy boat just across the dock from where Gerome was. Tucker relayed the information so Gerome would know he had company close by and could be careful getting away.

He took a deep breath, trying not to prance or pace as he did when he was nervous. He didn't want anything to happen to Gerome, so he kept watching, hoping Gerome would just return and they could get out of there.

"I'll only be a minute," a rough voice said. Tucker glanced in that direction. Bobby Ramone came down the ramp approaching the dock. Tucker sent a message, shoved the phone into his pocket, and picked up the tackle box. He headed the opposite way from Ramone's boat.

"Hey," he called, and Tucker froze. "Do you have the time?"

Tucker checked the phone. "Ten till five," he answered. Then he continued on, checking various boats. As soon as the coast was clear, he went back down the dock and out to the car, climbed inside, and locked the doors, keeping low to watch for Gerome.

He didn't return.

Tucker waited and waited. Bobby Ramone came back down the dock and got into the truck parked right next to him. Tucker curled up on the floor out of sight until the truck pulled away. He sent another message and waited for a reply but didn't receive one.

Tucker got out of the truck to try to get a better look, but he didn't see anyone out and about. He hoped to hell that Gerome wasn't lying hurt somewhere or, worse, floating in the marina. He needed to find out what was going on, so he left the truck and walked back down the dock, passing Ramone's boat. When he didn't see anything, he continued to the end of the dock and then, without knowing what else to do, returned to the truck. He had just gotten inside when the phone vibrated.

I'm okay. I'll be there in a few minutes. There were no other messages.

Chapter 7

"GOD, WHAT a mess," Gerome said under his breath. The thought of touching the stuff in here made him want to wash his hands until they were raw before he came in contact with any of the guys. He should have brought some fucking gloves… or maybe a whole box. Pushing that aside, he started at one end and searched methodically, working his way from the back to the front.

He lifted the top of one of the banquette seats for the dining table and groaned at the brick wrapped in plastic shrink wrap as well as a few "sample" bags. He grabbed one and slipped it into his pocket. Gerome was just disposing of the brick when his phone beeped with a message. He lowered the lid and put the cushion back into place. Gerome had a few seconds to get off the boat in time and turned to the stairs to get out.

A small group of papers caught his attention, and he reached for them and read the first few lines. He felt himself pale and his feet refused to move. Gerome took a deep breath as he stared into his worst nightmare.

Time was running out. He folded the papers and shoved them in his pocket.

Gerome was grateful for Tucker's message but realized he was now a sitting duck. He looked around and knew he had to think fast. If he were found on the boat, that would be the end. God knows what would happen.

He thought of diving off the side and swimming for it, but that would make too much noise, and Ramone was getting closer by the second. Out of options, he grabbed a plastic bag from the table, shoved his phone into it, jammed the bag into his pocket with the papers, and climbed over the front of the boat, lowering himself into the water, hanging on to one of the bumpers on the side away from the dock. Gerome closed his eyes and steadied his breathing as he waited.

He didn't have long to wait. Heavy footsteps on the deck above warned him of Bobby's presence. God, he hoped to hell he wasn't going to be staying long and that he didn't look out one of the portholes on that side. Though Gerome did his best to stay out of view.

His clothes grew heavier and his arms ached, but he continued holding on as Ramone rummaged around inside the boat. Gerome needed to keep a cool head and think. It might be possible to drop completely into the water and quietly swim away, but then he would need to get the hell out, and with his luck the way it was running, he'd climb out right in front of Bobby Ramone.

His arms felt like they were on fire, and he wished he could get a perch on something with his feet, but flailing around would only draw attention, so he needed to just stay where he was and hope.

A phone rang inside.

"Yeah. I'm coming."

Gerome rested his head on the fiberglass of the boat, willing the bastard to hurry up. Footsteps sounded once again, and Gerome waited, hoping to hell that Bobby Ramone didn't decide to walk to this side of the boat. All he would need to do was look down and Gerome would be in deep shit.

Chapter 8

WHEN GEROME came down the dock, his lower half was wet and he was dripping everywhere. Tucker opened the door and Gerome climbed right inside, squelching a little as he sat down.

"What happened?"

"I had just enough time to hang out of sight off the front of the boat while he got what he needed. The problem was that it wasn't as easy to get back in. I managed eventually." He started the engine and they hurried back toward the apartment.

"Did you find what you were looking for?" Tucker asked.

"Some of it, yeah." He seemed a little confused. "I'm going to take a shower and call the guys. I need their help figuring all this out. Go ahead and get yourself some dinner, and I'll call you a little later." Gerome pulled into his parking spot. "Thank you for your help. You were awesome." He turned off the engine and got out.

Tucker followed. "Do you really think that you get to make me worry myself raw for half an hour after I kept watch for you, did the whole lookout thing, and then when we get back here, you say thanks and go inside?" He tapped his foot. "You go get a shower and warmed up, and I'll be over in fifteen minutes. I want to know what happened and what's going on. It was my stupidity that got us mixed up in this mess, but I want to help get out of it."

Gerome glared at him, his expression stony, and Tucker half expected him to shut him out, but eventually Gerome sighed and nodded. "Fine. Be here in ten minutes. I'll have the guys order pizza and stuff, and once we're done talking, we'll ask Cheryl and Joshie to come over and eat." He stomped inside the apartment, closing the door harder than was necessary.

"What's going on?" Cheryl asked when Tucker joined her and Joshie in the apartment.

"Why is Mr. Gerome mad? He slammed the door," Joshie asked as he stared up at Tucker. "If you were bad, you should say sorry."

"It's okay. He's the one who was naughty," Tucker said, sharing a wink with Joshie. "And to make up for it, he and his friends are going to order pizza, and they invited all of us."

"Is that what you were fighting about?" Cheryl asked, confused.

Tucker shook his head. "He went onto Ramone's boat, and I think he might have found something that disturbed him. I don't know what it is. He wants to talk about it with the guys, but apparently they're going to get pizza. So you and Joshie should come over at six thirty. I'm going over to find out what's going on."

"Okay. We'll be over. Do you know if Coby will be there? Joshie has been asking to play with him for days." She yawned and sat down once again.

"I'll ask. Just sit and rest until you're ready to come over." Tucker checked the time, went across the hall, and knocked on Gerome's door.

"Go on in," Richard said as he approached with an armload of beer. "In fact, open the door for me. Terrance is on his way, and Daniel will be around soon enough with Coby, and the boys can play." Tucker opened the door, and Richard followed him inside. "Gerome, I'm here with Tucker, so get your ass out here," Richard called. "That is, if you want any of the beer. If Terrance gets to it first, there won't be much left." He laughed, popped two open, and handed one to Tucker.

"You're a regular fucking comedian," Gerome said as he came in barefoot in pants and a T-shirt that showed off his chest and arms. Tucker handed him the beer and opened another one. Gerome sat on the sofa and tugged Tucker down next to him.

"What did you find?" Tucker asked, his patience wearing thin. "Was it more of the bundles he wanted me to find?"

"No. There was nothing like that on board. The boat was a disorganized mess. Whoever lives there is a total slob." He stood and laid some soggy papers on the counter. "They got a little wet."

"Are drug runners keeping records and doing paperwork?" Richard asked as he got up to look. He and Gerome shared a silence, both of them growing pale.

The communication between them was clear, but only to the two of them. Tucker knew something was going on. "I see." He leaned closer.

"I also found this," Gerome said and handed Richard a plastic bag. "There was a lot more, but it all ended up in the water." He grinned.

"Are those drugs?" Tucker asked. "Should we taste them like they do on TV?"

Gerome chuckled. "That's something that only exists on TV. You can't tell by taste, and what if it's a type of poison?" He shrugged. "No one will be tasting it, and yes, I do believe this is cocaine. And before the night is over, we will be getting rid of it." He set down the small plastic bag.

"How much did you dispose of?" Richard said as Terrance came inside. Gerome got Terrance a beer and brought him up to date.

"So we've got some drug running going on," Terrance said with a shrug. "Why do we care or want to get involved? Call the police, let them deal with it, and then this can be over. They'll arrest this guy and he'll be gone." It seemed like a pretty good idea to Tucker, but Gerome showed him one of the wet pages, and Terrance grew quiet. "I still say we leave it up to the police. It's their job." Terrance grabbed a beer and flopped onto the sofa, putting his feet on the coffee table.

"Yeah, you should do that," Tucker agreed. "But Gerome was on that boat, and I was seen on the dock. What if they come looking for us?" He met the gaze of each of them. "I don't want to be hauled off to jail because I was there. I'm a homeless guy. People like to blame guys like me for everything." He didn't like this at all.

Gerome, Richard, and Terrance all got that same "ESP" look. "I think Tucker is right," Richard explained. "But we all need to stay away from these people. No more breaking into boats or following folks around the key. If we see something, call the police and let them handle it. We all want to stay out of this and away from any sort of trouble, especially this kind." Clearly he was a little spooked. He seemed paler than normal, even now.

"Fine," Gerome snapped. "But you know guys like this don't stop. They keep coming, and though so far Tucker has been lucky, it isn't going to stay that way."

Richard's gaze scanned the room like radar. "We need to stay away from this if we possibly can."

Terrance nodded, and after hesitating, Gerome did as well. The tension in the room seemed to pull the walls in, making the space smaller and more confining.

"We may not have a choice," Gerome countered. Both Terrance and Richard nodded. It was like the three of them were speaking in code, with hidden meanings everywhere. Not that it was really any of Tucker's business.

"Stop this," Tucker interrupted. "Look, if Cheryl and I are going to be this much trouble, we should just move on. We got along before without the three of you, and we'll be okay again. It's that simple. We'll pack our stuff and be out of here tomorrow. We can leave town and go somewhere else completely. Maybe farther down south or something."

Gerome sat next down next to him and put an arm around his shoulder. "You don't want to leave. We aren't arguing about you and Cheryl." He sighed and turned to Richard as though he wasn't sure what to say.

Richard in turn glanced at Terrance. Tucker got the feeling that more of that silent communication was winging its way through the room. Finally Terrance shrugged. "The three of us have a history, that's pretty plain, and, well, that history and your current predicament seem to have been drawn in together."

"Have you met Ramone before?" Tucker asked.

Richard shook his head. "No." None of them seemed to know what to say.

A knock on the door interrupted the tension. Daniel and Coby came inside, followed by Cheryl and Joshie. Richard, Terrance, and Gerome seemed almost relieved, and Tucker was just as confused as he ever had been. Something was definitely going on, and his curiosity about what Gerome and his friends were hiding grew more acute. Not that people didn't have a right to their privacy, but suddenly it seemed that what they were keeping a secret affected his and possibly Cheryl and Joshie's safety. He wished they would be honest with him.

Bobby Ramone was a bad guy, that was obvious, and if these three were afraid of him, there had to be some connection. They weren't police; Tucker was sure of that. Maybe they were ex-military and couldn't leave well enough alone. Maybe something like the A-Team. He dismissed that notion pretty quickly. These guys were different from that, even. He just couldn't figure out what it was. Tucker thought the best thing to do for right now was to watch and pretend he was taking everything at face value and continue to go along. Maybe what he'd thought in the very first place was correct. Maybe you didn't get something for nothing, and the price of Gerome's help hadn't been named yet.

TERRANCE HAD ordered pizza, and the delivery guy arrived. Coby and Joshie sat at the counter eating while the others filled the drab seating area. Gerome's furniture reminded Tucker of what was in the apartment he and Cheryl were sharing, and he wondered where on earth it had been purchased—maybe uglyfurniture.com? At least the idea put his curiosity about Gerome and his friends at bay… for like thirty seconds.

"Thank you for having us over," Cheryl said between nibbles on her slice of pizza. "Joshie has been asking to play with Coby for days now." She smiled and set her plate down on the coffee table.

"It's no problem. Coby has been asking the same." The two boys had their heads together. They were adorable. Tucker wondered how much longer the two of them would sit and eat before they began running the cars and trucks along the floor.

"If it's okay, I'm going to go back and lie down for a while," Cheryl said, patting Tucker on the shoulder. "Will you watch him?"

"Of course," Tucker agreed, and Cheryl left after giving Joshie a quick kiss on the top of the head. He watched her go, biting his lower lip.

"You're worried about her," Gerome said.

Tucker nodded. "She's been really tired and listless for days now. I thought it was because she'd been ill, but she says she feels okay. And yet she sleeps so much. She worked today, and that must have wiped her out." At least he hoped that was all it was.

"Have you talked to her?" Gerome asked gently.

He shrugged. "She says she's fine and just needs a chance to catch up on her rest. Sleeping in a tent all the time isn't the best recipe for quality relaxation. The camp really never quieted down, and though most people learn to sleep even with the noise, it isn't really restful." He still would have expected her to have been able to get over this. "I asked about finding a doctor, and she said she was fine and that I shouldn't worry."

"Then there isn't much you can do," Gerome said. "Just keep an eye on her, and hopefully this will pass. Maybe she isn't used to working. Today was her first day, and she was probably really busy. There's been a lot of change for all of you, and that can take a lot out of some people." He got up. "Do you want another piece?" Gerome got them each another slice of the pepperoni and mushroom.

Tucker hoped Gerome was right. "I guess I'm just worried," he said. "She didn't eat very much either."

"Maybe she had something at the restaurant before she came home," Gerome offered, and that made sense. Tucker just wished he could shake the uneasiness that seemed to surround him. Gerome was a great guy, kind and strong, and Tucker really wanted to be able to trust him, but there were too many things left unsaid. They left Tucker wondering what was coming next.

"Look what Coby gave me," Joshie said as he hurried over, a Matchbox car clutched in his hand. "He's nice."

Tucker turned to Daniel, who nodded. "We went through some of his toys, and Coby wanted Joshie to have something to play with," Daniel explained. "I also went through some of Coby's clothes, since Joshie is a little smaller than him, and I have a bag of things that should probably fit him in the car. Coby is growing so fast right now that I swear I'm getting him new clothes all the time."

Tucker smiled and nodded. It sucked to be poor and not be able to afford the most basic things for the important people in his life. "Thank you." It bothered him. Not that Daniel wasn't nice. His actions were out of kindness. What pissed Tucker off was the fact that the kindness was necessary. Cheryl should be able to provide for Joshie, and in a fair world, she'd be able to, and the help that she needed to do that would be available. As it was, all three of them had fallen through the cracks of a system that was supposed to help them but only put obstacles in their way.

"Do you want some more pizza?" Gerome asked as he got up to grab a beer.

Tucker shook his head and asked for some water. His maudlin mood seemed to have taken over, and he figured it must be because of the beer. He hated feeling this way. But damn it all, he knew where he stood when he was in the tent camp and on his own. He knew what and who he could rely on. Now, just days removed from that, he was more frightened than he had been there because he had something to lose. They all did. Joshie was making friends. The delighted laughter from the floor was one of the best sounds he had heard in a long time. Somehow he had to make this continue.

But all the secrets and unsaid things he'd run into in the last few hours made him wonder just who these guys were. It all came back to what they wanted from him… and from Cheryl. He knew that Bobby Ramone was either running drugs or working for someone who was. Did that mean that these three were part of a rival organization? Were they keeping him safe so he didn't fall into the hands of a rival? That didn't make much sense, and Tucker dismissed it. He had nothing anyone could want. Tucker didn't even know anything, and yet these guys had protected him. Well, Gerome had done the protecting, but it seemed Richard and Terrance had Gerome's back. This entire situation was like the weirdest four-gy he had ever heard of.

"It's going to be okay," Gerome whispered when he sat back down and handed him the water.

He tried to put aside some of his concerns for now. There was nothing he could do about any of it at the moment, especially not with Joshie in the room. "What bothers me is that I had nothing to do with anything. I didn't do anything, didn't find anything, and yet I seem to be in the middle of this." He sipped his water and sat back, searching his mind for anything he might have missed. He was nearly completely in the dark about all of this. Shit, he should have simply walked away when he had the chance. Instead, desperation had driven him to do something completely stupid. He wanted to go back to the apartment, where he could think straight. It was more than a little difficult with Gerome sitting right next to him, his leg pressed right next to Gerome's, their shoulders bumping every once in a while. And damn, when the air circulation in the room was just right, Gerome's scent filled his nose, and his mouth went dry at the heady scent. Talk about losing the ability to think straight.

"How are things at the hardware store?" Tucker asked Terrance.

He shrugged. "The same as always." He leaned forward. "Though I did have a couple of kids come in today. I think they were trying to play a joke on one of the other associates. They were asking for hammer without the claw on the end. When she explained that it was a ball-peen hammer, they all started to giggle. They must have been ten or so." Terrance smiled. He was quite handsome when he did that. Not as sexy as Gerome, but a smile was a good look for him.

"Terrance…." Richard's tone was cautionary.

"I came around the corner, put my hands on my hips, and glared at the three of them. I swear one of them might have peed himself, and all three of them turned tail and ran out of there like their pants were on fire. Gina and I got a laugh out of it after they were gone."

Tucker rolled his eyes. "You enjoy scaring children? Maybe you should be Scrooge in the town Christmas play."

Gerome choked and coughed. "No, the Ghost of Christmas Future in those black robes. They'll swear he's the angel of death."

"You're both nuts," Terrance grumped, folding his arms over his chest. "And for the record, yes, I like scaring children who misbehave. It's my calling in life."

"You're not scary," Coby pronounced. "Just mean-looking sometimes." He went back to playing, and all the guys cracked up, except Terrance, who tried to hold a grumpy expression before smiling himself. Joshie looked up, watching them all as though they were crazy, before going back to playing with the trucks.

"I guess that's the last word on that subject," Gerome teased. "How are things working out at the restaurant?"

Richard grinned. "The problems we've been having in the kitchen seem to have worked their way out." He winked at Tucker. "Zane never seems to get along with anyone. The number of people that we've gone through in the kitchen has been ridiculous. He really seems to have calmed down the past few days."

Tucker put his hands up. "I had nothing to do with that." He had just been doing his job.

"Right. You do your job well and seem to know what needs to be done. And thank God Zane stopped ranting and raving about his salads and soups. Alan and I were beginning to wonder if we were going to have to take the guy out back for another talking-to pretty soon. Then you showed up and the kitchen settled into a good place. He actually smiles now."

Tucker chuckled. "Yeah, I didn't know it was possible."

"Neither did we," Richard told him. "He says you have real talent, and Zane never says nice things about people."

Tucker leaned forward a little. "What is he doing here? Not that there's anything wrong with the Driftwood, but it seems like he could work at a high-end restaurant. There are advanced skills there, and yet he's working at the Driftwood."

"Family commitments," Richard answered. "I'm not at liberty to talk about it, because it's his business, but I think that's part of his frustration. Zane would really like to create fancier dishes, but the clientele isn't going to allow for that."

Tucker shrugged. "Why not as specials?" he asked. "Folks are always looking for something different every now and then. I mentioned that he should talk to you and Alan about it. I don't know if that's the kind of thing you want to do, but…."

Richard sat back. "So that's where that idea came from? Alan said that they used to do that but stopped at some point. We think it's a good idea and told Zane to go ahead."

That was awesome. Tucker thought Zane just needed to be able to stretch himself a little. Everyone needed a chance to do something out of the ordinary every once in a while, and Zane was no different. The chef at Tucker's last job had loved developing new dishes and specials more than anything else. "Good. I think there are things I can learn from him."

"And then maybe you can run a kitchen of your own someday," Richard told him. "You do good work and you learn fast. That says a lot."

"I like what we're doing," Tucker said, and he lightly bumped Gerome's shoulder, knowing he was the one who had brought his abilities to Richard and Alan's attention. He really felt like he was making a contribution.

"That's good." Richard glanced around, and Daniel joined him, the two getting close on the chair.

"I should probably get Joshie home and ready for bed." He also wanted to check on Cheryl.

Gerome put an arm around his shoulder, leaning in close. "Will I see you later?"

Tucker wasn't sure how to answer. Yes, he did want to spend time with Gerome, but all the topics that the guys skirted around had him wondering. He needed some time to think, and that wasn't possible around Gerome.

"I need to see how Cheryl is and get Joshie to bed. Can I let you know?" Tucker asked, and Gerome nodded. He got Joshie, who said goodbye to Daniel and thanked Coby for the car before they walked across the hall, doubts ringing through Tucker's head.

Chapter 9

GEROME SHOOK his head as Daniel gathered his and Coby's things before leaning in close to Richard. "Don't be too late." He kissed him, and Coby hugged Richard goodbye before leaving.

"This is going to be real trouble," Terrance said as soon as the door clicked closed. "All they need to do is send someone down here to clean up this mess, someone who knows who we are, and all of us are completely screwed. Richard and Daniel most of all." He glared at Gerome so hard Gerome was surprised Terrance didn't burn a hole through him. "You had to get involved, and now we're closer to the Garvic operation than we have been since we left Detroit."

"How was I to know?" Gerome jumped to his feet, growling back at Terrance.

"Keep your voices down," Richard cautioned. "These places aren't exactly soundproof. "And for the record, Gerome didn't know. All he did was stand up to a bully."

"For a guy he thought was cute," Terrance sneered.

"Quit acting like an asshole," Gerome countered. "Just because you don't have anyone interested in you."

Terrance scoffed. "Please. I can get any guy I want, any time. I have people lined up for this." He motioned to himself. "But I have better things to do right now than screw half of Longboat Key. I need to keep the two of you in line, because both of you seem to fall for the first guy to come along, and then we all have to clean up the mess."

"Terrance," Richard said calmly, but Gerome could tell by the vein in his neck that he was ready to explode. "Would you not want Coby calling you Uncle Terry?" He was pulling out the big guns. Coby had all of them wrapped around his little finger, and he did it so easily. If Gerome was honest with himself, Joshie was well on his way to doing the same thing.

"Fuck you," Terrance swore, without much heat. "Fine. Then you tell me what we're going to do with a damned brick of their money in the closet and Garvic's people in the area doing business. We could hand the money over to Elizabeth and let her deal with it from here. But you know Garvic Junior isn't going to stop looking for us, and if anyone gets even a whiff that we're here, they'll descend on us like no tomorrow." His expression softened. "It would rip everything apart for Richard and Daniel if we had to move again. They have lives here—we all do to a degree."

Gerome had to agree. “But Garvic’s people would be here regardless of what I did for Tucker. Instead, we know about it now and can figure something out. Bobby Ramone is a low-level operative who is probably going to end up dead very soon. No one loses that much money and gets away with it.”

“And he has to know that,” Richard added, which only circled things right back to Tucker.

“So Ramone is going to be hunting Tucker even more intensely,” Gerome interjected. “Maybe we should arrange for the money to appear in his boat. He’ll have what he wants and maybe he’ll stop hunting for Tucker.”

Richard shook his head. “Nope. Money or not, they are going to work to cut any ties that anyone has to their activity. If they think Tucker could have any idea about what’s happening, they are never going to let him walk away from anything. As long as he can tell anyone what he knows—or might know—or even suspects….”

Gerome swore under his breath. “And all because I got to the bundle first and didn’t just leave it there.” The old truth that he simply shouldn’t get involved was most definitely kicking him in the ass right now. Tucker could have found the bundle, handed it over, been paid, and that could have been that. Of course, then Gerome never would have met Tucker, or Joshie and Cheryl. Gerome didn’t like that idea.

“Hey,” Richard snapped. “Going back over the shit that’s happened doesn’t help any of us. Right now we’re safe, and we need to figure out how to stay that way. And I think the best thing to do is put an end to the drug running that’s going on just off the coast. We’re going to have to watch the beach and report what we see. Harass them into moving on.”

"And how do we do that?" Terrance asked snidely.

Richard shrugged. "I think Gerome needs to make a call to Elizabeth, explain what he saw, and that we believe it's continuing. Let her turn this all over to DEA, and they can clean up the mess. It's what they're supposed to do."

"Yeah," Gerome said. "Except I have nothing to go on except a bundle of cash that we're not supposed to have and something I saw once. It may never happen again, and I have no idea when these guys will make their runs. It will be like looking for a needle in a haystack. Who knows if they'll get anywhere?" He sighed. "I guess I'll need to hang out on the beach some more and hope I see something."

"Maybe take someone with you to make the time speed by," Richard said quietly.

Terrance groaned but let the subject drop. "What are we going to do about him?"

"He doesn't know anything," Gerome said.

Terrance shook his head. "Don't be so sure about that. Tucker isn't dumb, and we can talk around our past all we want. He's curious; I could see it in his eyes." He gathered up the empty pizza boxes. "You gotta deal with this somehow."

"I know, and I'll figure it out," Gerome said. He wasn't sure what he was going to tell him. Terrance was right. He needed to develop a cover story.

"Just tell him something close to the truth. That you have a past that isn't pretty and it's hard to talk about. Everyone has a past that they wish they could run away from. I bet Tucker does as well. Be enigmatic and as nonthreatening as possible."

"Yeah, like that's going to work." Gerome realized that he needed to deal with this and that it was his responsibility. "I'll take care of it." He put his hand up to stop further discussion, because it wasn't going to be helpful.

"Just one more question. Do you really like this guy?" Terrance asked. "I mean really like him, like he could be the one, the way Daniel was for Richard?" He groaned. "Like I said before, we are all so damned screwed." He sighed.

"And why is that?" Richard asked, crossing his arms.

"Because the more people who know about us—and if Gerome is in love, then at some point he's going to have to explain who we are—the more likely it is that eventually someone will say something and our lives will end up in the 'wheel of towns to move to' lottery all over again." Terrance growled. "You're going to make me say it, aren't you?"

Gerome crossed his arms over his chest just like Richard.

"You're both bastards, you know that? Fine. I kind of like it here and don't want to end up freezing my butt off in Idaho or stuck in some quaint little seaside village in Maine… where we still freeze our asses off for half the year."

"Then help us," Gerome said.

Terrance rolled his eyes. "I always help you. Richard got Daniel because I helped, and maybe you'll end up with Tucker… or some other guy… because I helped. And I end up with nothing." For a second he looked like he was twelve years old. Gerome lowered his arms and patted Terrance on the shoulder. "I don't need your pity or any of that shit."

Gerome and Richard shared a look and then both shook their heads at the same time.

"Fine. Just quit that silent eyebrow code shit and figure this stuff out."

Gerome sighed. "We're going to watch and see if we can figure out more about what's going on."

"And we all keep an eye out for Tucker," Richard added.

Gerome wished to hell that their lives were simpler. There was something to be said about what they'd had in Detroit. At least they all knew where they stood and understood their lives. Being out here in the law-abiding world was so much harder. Keeping hidden from their old lives while somehow trying to build new ones. And every time something good happened, it was always filtered through the threat of exposure and the fact that their old lives were just sitting there, waiting to take away whatever they might have built.

"Yeah." Gerome held out his hand, and Richard took it. So did Terrance. "We need to keep the people we care about safe. That's how we've always done things." He turned to Terrance. "Right?"

"And you really care about Tucker that much?" Terrance pressed.

Gerome stared, not looking away from his gaze for a second. "I don't know what's going on exactly." He certainly wasn't going to spill his feelings about Tucker to Terrance before he had had a chance to talk things over with him. Gerome was a little confused as far as his feelings went. Things with Tucker were very different from anything he'd experienced before. "But I want a fucking chance to try to figure it out."

Terrance gripped his hand. "Okay. That's good enough for me." Sometimes the level of trust between all of them struck Gerome hard. They might argue and bicker with each other—they'd always done it—but in the end they arrived at better decisions because of it. "We always have each other's back, no matter what."

"Yeah, we do," Richard added as he released his grip. "But that doesn't mean that we aren't careful."

"What are you thinking?"

"That I need Daniel to try to find out what information we can about Tucker."

Gerome wasn't happy and tried to disguise his tension.

"We need to know that there isn't some hidden agenda."

"From a man who spent months, if not longer, living in a tent, half-starved and desperate enough to take a job to scour the beach for a package just for a few hundred dollars?" He cocked his eyebrows as though it were a ridiculous notion, but figured it wasn't going to hurt anything, and if it put some of Terrance and Richard's doubts to rest, then that would be good.

"You never know. Things could simply be exactly as they appear, or they could be more. I don't really know. And neither do you," Richard added. "Let's be cautious here, and let's find out what the hell is going on so we can put an end to it and get this threat to all of us as far away as possible."

Now that was something they could all agree on.

Richard headed for the door, with Terrance behind him. Gerome said good night and closed the door after them, realizing that Terrance had somehow grabbed the last beer on his way out.

GEROME SAT on the sofa with the television on, but he wasn't paying attention. He thought of wandering down to the beach to watch the waves, but realistically, that was a futile exercise. He couldn't constantly stake out the beach to try to figure out when a rendezvous might take place. They didn't even know if there *would* be another one.

Footsteps sounded outside the door, and Gerome tensed, hoping it was Tucker. But there was no further sound, and he sank a little more into loneliness.

What the hell had happened to him? Gerome used to enjoy being by himself. He got so little time alone with his two friends working with him on a constant basis. They had been in each other's business and at each other's apartments all the time. Now Richard had Daniel and a family of his own, and Terrance worked two jobs and was gone a lot. Consequently, Gerome had plenty of time on his hands.

With a sigh, he pushed himself out of the chair, went to the door, and stepped into the hall. He was tempted to knock on Tucker's door, but he didn't want to wake Joshie and…. This was stupid. He turned to go inside as the door opened.

"Gerome?" Tucker said softly. "What are you doing out here?" He stepped into the hallway and closed the door.

Gerome shrugged because he didn't want to seem like an idiot. "I thought I heard something." That was a good cover, even if it sounded lame. "But I guess it was nothing. I didn't mean to disturb you." He was just going a little stir-crazy and needed to get outside. "Are Joshie and Cheryl asleep?"

"Yeah. They're both out like lights. I was going to watch TV, but Joshie is a light sleeper and it would wake him up. I tried to read but didn't have a great deal of luck with that either." He sighed slightly. "I was going to come over, but then I wasn't sure if I should and if it was a good time. I know you needed to talk with the guys, and…." He shrugged. "It felt different, and I didn't know what you wanted me to do."

"How about we go for a walk?" Gerome asked.

"That's not a bad idea. I could use the chance to clear my head," Tucker said. He went back into the apartment and grabbed an old sweatshirt from inside the door. Then he closed it again, and Gerome motioned him forward.

Gerome grabbed his keys and checked the door before catching up to Tucker and taking his hand. They didn't talk about where they were going but ended up going toward the beach, the lap of the waves on the sand getting louder the closer they got.

"I always come down here when I need to think," Gerome admitted.

"Me too. There's something about the sound of the water that relaxes me and gets my head working." Tucker squeezed his hand. "I don't come down here very much after dark. I like walking on the beach at twilight. I'm usually afraid that I'll trip or something."

Tucker took his arm, and they slowly navigated the sand. There wasn't a great deal of light. A few of the homes had lights on the beach side, and that provided just enough light for them to see.

"Yeah." Gerome wasn't thinking of anything right now but where Tucker held his hand and how close he was. The water was dark, and there was no activity tonight. The beach was deserted, as Gerome would have expected. It seemed like he and Tucker had the entire space to themselves. "Maybe it's like getting back to nature, but the water seems to touch my soul." There had been a time when he didn't think he had one.

"When I first met Cheryl and Joshie, we were all living near the beach. It was just close enough that we could hear the waves at night." Tucker tightened his hold, and Gerome slowed his steps. "I was so scared. I had no idea what was going to happen to me. I'd lost my job and my apartment, and I had little idea how I was going to feed myself. There had already been some nights when I had gone without eating." They came to a stop, and Gerome gently tugged his arm away from Tucker's and put it around him instead. "I can still remember lying in that little tent, in complete darkness, just me, my thoughts, and the sound of the waves." He shivered, and Gerome slowly turned them around, heading back the way they'd come.

"I can't imagine how that would feel," Gerome began. "No… I guess that's not really true. I know what it feels like to wonder if you have a future at all." He turned to Tucker. "I had no one, just like you did… at least it felt that way. In some ways that fear stayed with me for years."

"But you had the guys, Richard and Terrance," Tucker said.

Gerome nodded. "It was still hard being a foster kid, shuffled from place to place because you weren't really wanted." He sighed softly. "Maybe that isn't exactly true." He paused as his own childhood came into focus in a way it never had before. "Maybe I never allowed myself to be cared for. I don't really know."

Tucker leaned closer, his arms encircling Gerome's waist. "Just tell me and get it off your chest."

Gerome shrugged. He hadn't come out here for a heart-to-heart talk or to bare his soul, but that seemed to be what was happening… and he wasn't too sure how comfortable he was about it. His head whirled for a few seconds, and then his thoughts settled into calmness. Maybe he'd been carrying this around for so long that it was time for him to let it go. "Maybe I was shuffled and moved all the time because I never gave any of them a chance. I wonder sometimes if I had been more open to them, if some of my foster families would have been more open to me. I kept myself closed off and aloof, even aggressive, just to hold most of the world at bay."

"So you couldn't be hurt again?" Tucker finished, and Gerome nodded. "And you've been doing that for a long time."

Gerome couldn't disagree. "I think all three of us have, to some degree."

"Did you have anyone you were close to besides Richard and Terrance?" Tucker asked.

Gerome turned out toward the water. "I did. Terrance's mother. She died over a year ago." He thanked God every time he remembered that he and the guys had been able to talk to her before then. Gerome hugged Tucker tighter and closed his eyes. "There were many times in my life that I have been alone."

"But you always had the guys?"

"Since we were about eight years old, yeah. They are my family, like brothers."

Tucker chuckled, and Gerome wondered what he had said that could possibly have been funny. "Did you ever think it strange that all three of you are gay?"

Gerome had never thought about it. For each of them, it was just a part of themselves that always was. "I think we ended up together *because* we were gay. All of us were different otherwise, and maybe we were drawn together. We were tough kids and we lived in a rough place."

"Is that why you three can look at each other and seem to communicate without words?" Tucker asked. "I've seen that when you guys get together."

Gerome nodded. "We have so much shared experience, I guess. Most of the time I don't even think we realize we're doing it." He tried to keep his voice level, knowing this was his chance to smooth over any suspicions Tucker might have. He wasn't sure if it would work, but he was sure that making too much of what they had seen and now knew about the people involved in the drug running offshore was only going to raise Tucker's suspicions, and he didn't want to do that. All of them relied on staying under the radar for safety, and when Gerome had stepped in to help Tucker, he hadn't anticipated that his act of kindness could severely blow back on all of them. And yet, if he hadn't stepped in, then he wouldn't have Tucker in his arms right now, and that felt so right.

Gerome leaned closer, touching his lips to Tucker's, who shifted in his arms, pressing against him, their kiss growing more heated by the second. Tucker slipped his arms around Gerome's neck, claiming his mouth with an overwhelming amount of power, filling Gerome with heat that even the breeze off the water couldn't cool. His heart raced, and his attention narrowed only to the places where they touched. He wanted to lower Tucker to the sand, cradle him, and take him right here and now.

He forced himself to pull away, breathing deeply, his chest expanding as though he had run a marathon. The cool sea breeze did nothing to cut the raging fire that went through him. "I think you and I should get off the beach and go home." He looked up from over

Tucker's shoulder and paused. "Turn around," Gerome said. Tucker did, and he nuzzled up right behind him.

"What are we looking at?"

"The boat lights," Gerome said.

Tucker craned to look at him. "Do you think…?" He shifted his gaze back out to sea, and Gerome watched as the lights of the boats came closer. Like before, they were just offshore. "Wow, anyone can see them."

"Yeah. But no one is going to think twice about some lights offshore. There are a ton of boats all over there, so there is nothing out of the ordinary." Gerome listened for any sound on the wind but heard nothing but the breeze. The boats came together, and Gerome craned his head to try to make out any details.

"We should go," Tucker said and turned, striding off the beach. "We need to get back to your car."

"Why?" Gerome asked.

"If they came out of the bay, there's only one bridge that they could pass under on their way out, and if they turn around, they have to pass under the same bridge. We can actually get a look at the boat to verify its name." He walked faster, and Gerome hurried to catch up.

They raced back to the apartment, and Gerome got his keys. They headed out as quickly as he dared. He didn't want to get a ticket and be delayed, so he kept it a little slower than he wanted. The bridge was a few miles down.

"Do you think we made it in time?" Tucker asked.

"I would think so. We can move faster on the road than they can on water. I would think we beat them unless they turned around right after we left. Who knows?" He came to the bridge, drove over it, and pulled off the side of the road. Gerome and Tucker both got out of the car and hurried onto the bridge. “Look.” Lights disappeared into the bay side, a small craft probably having passed under the bridge a few seconds before they arrived.

“We’re too late,” Tucker said, his shoulders slumping.

“Maybe not. We don’t know if that’s the same boat.” Gerome steered Tucker to the other side of the bridge. “We can wait here a few minutes to see if any other craft come in from that direction. That seemed really quick for them.” But he wasn’t sure, and as they watched, time ticked away.

Gerome was beginning to think Tucker was right when the throaty call of an engine drifted on the wind.

“Get down,” Gerome said, crouching behind the railing and one of the posts. “It’s best if they don’t know they’re being watched.”

Tucker did the same as the boat grew nearer. Gerome watched through one of the openings in the railing as the boat drew closer to the bridge and then passed under it. After checking for traffic, he hurried to the other side, trying to get a look at the back of the boat. Just as he crouched down, the lights on the boat flipped out, denying him the information he was hoping for.

“Did you get the name of the boat?” Gerome asked.

“*Flying Rage*,” Tucker said. “I saw it just before the lights went out. Not the same boat.”

Gerome shook his head. “Nope. This one is bigger, with a lot more storage space.” He waited until the boat was far enough away, then stood, watching the boat as long as he could to get some sort of idea on where it might be headed.

"The other side of the bay. They must dock on the mainland side." He groaned softly. "At least we know the name of the boat." He stood and held out his hand, Tucker's slipping into his. "I don't know what we're going to do with it." He walked toward the car, missing Tucker's warm hand in his when he let go to get in. Gerome turned the car around and slowly drove back toward home, checking his mirrors in case they had picked up some unwanted interest.

"What do we know?" Tucker asked.

Gerome chuckled. "Not a hell of a lot. Two boats met out on the gulf, and one returned to the key under the bridge. I don't know if they were picking up or dropping off. Hell, they could have been bringing someone back and just met to transfer passengers. I have no idea." He had to remind himself that he shouldn't know too much about the last meetup he'd witnessed. He hated keeping the bundle hiding in his kitchen a secret from Tucker. That bundle was trouble personified, but it was the only solid evidence they had that something was happening.

"But we know the name of the boat. Do you think you could sneak onto that one too and have a look around?" Tucker asked.

Gerome chuckled. "Damn, I think I'm being a bad influence on you." He smiled as they approached the apartment building. He pulled into his spot and got out of the car. "But we can probably find out where the boat is berthed and then take a look." He would have to be careful. The anchorages on the other side of the bay were smaller, and a lot of them attached directly to businesses or restaurants. That meant it was going to be more difficult to remain anonymous. Gerome was going to need to do some recon and figure out if it was even possible to look into this further. "But then we turn it over to the police and let them take it from there."

"Yeah. But we're gonna find out first." Tucker followed Gerome into the apartment. "This was really exciting."

"Tucker. We didn't really find out anything." There was nothing more they could figure out tonight.

"Sure we did. We know that someone is still using the waters off the coast for drug deals, and that someone is from the area. Do you think Bobby Ramone is behind this whole thing?"

Gerome shrugged. "Maybe." He tried to put the pieces together. It was pretty obvious that Ramone was partnering with members of the Garvic organization, which meant it was likely that drug trafficking had moved into the area, but he was hesitant to get involved. It could put all of them in jeopardy. "I think we should take everything we know and turn it over to the police. We can make a few calls and let them take it from here."

"But…."

Gerome tugged Tucker closer and instantly wondered if it was smart. "I know you think this is a good idea, but what if something goes wrong and you or I are seen? We could be followed back here, and that could put Joshie and Cheryl in danger." The idea to go after them was tempting. A little larceny and excitement in his life wasn't necessarily bad. Gerome sure as hell knew how to take care of himself. But there was more to think about than just himself.

"Maybe you're right," Tucker agreed softly. "This isn't some television show, and we're not amateur sleuths."

"Exactly. We should step back, turn over what we've seen to law enforcement, and let them handle it. They can investigate and figure out what's going on." Hopefully the people involved would be caught and put out of business, or scared off enough that they moved to a different area and left them alone. Either way, Gerome got the result he wanted. "You did great tonight," he added with a smile, gazing deeply into Tucker's eyes. "You thought quickly, and we got to the bridge in time."

"Yeah, but I really wanted to jump off the bridge onto the boat, catch those guys red-handed, and…." He grinned, and Gerome smiled as well.

"You're such a goof sometimes." He loved that Tucker could play with him and tease him. No one really did that. Gerome intimidated a lot of people, and it was nice that Tucker didn't feel that way.

"Come on," Tucker said, pulling away and taking him by the hand.

"Where are we going?"

Tucker rolled his eyes. "To the bedroom." His tone held an implied "duh," and Gerome followed behind him. "I liked you holding me on the beach… so let's go back to how that felt."

Gerome tugged Tucker into his arms, holding him tightly, bringing their lips together. He might have wondered if that was what Tucker wanted, but the soft moan told him he had received the message perfectly, and there were definitely times when talking was overrated.

GEROME WOULD never get tired of the deep, enticing sounds Tucker made in his throat. There was something about Tucker that made Gerome want more. Nothing was ever enough. After athletic sex, they had gone to sleep only to wake as a storm blew in, thunder rolling and rocking around them as Tucker climbed on top of him. God, that was amazing, and as Tucker sank down onto him, his breath hitched in the darkness, lightning flashing. Gerome's gasp was swallowed by the thunder as it shook the building. Or it could have been the desire that bloomed inside him that left Gerome quivering on the bed.

He lost track of the number of times he and Tucker came together in the night. Every time he rolled over, Tucker drew nearer, his lips finding Gerome's, and they started again. The night eventually quieted, and they slept until light streamed in the window.

Gerome sat up in bed, wiping his hands down his face, groaning as his muscles protested. He hoped to heck that Tucker wasn't sore, but that was probably wishful thinking.

Tucker's hair was all he could see poking out of the bedding. He didn't move, other than the covers slowly rising and falling. Gerome got up and went to the bathroom. He checked the clock as he passed, and after relieving himself, he returned to the bed for another hour. Tucker drew closer, humming softly in his sleep. Gerome closed his eyes and dozed, waking just before the alarm sounded.

"What time is it?" Tucker moaned softly, lifting his head. "Oh God, it's too early." He lay back down, covering his head with a groan.

"It's nearly eight."

"So?" came a muffled reply. "You had your way with me all night long. I need my rest." Tucker groaned and burrowed under the covers. "A guy can only take so much passion, and then he needs some sleep."

"If I remember, you were the one who—"

Tucker laughed and burrowed closer. "Yeah, I know." He lifted his head once again, eyes shining. "You were amazing." He rested his head on Gerome's chest, and Gerome gently stroked his shoulder. He liked this, just some time for the two of them to be together. Gerome was still satiated, and before—back in Detroit—that would have meant getting the guy who warmed his bed out the door as quickly as possible. Now all he wanted was to lie here with Tucker in the quiet, only the two of them, with the rest of the world outside the door… and it could stay there, as far as he was concerned.

"Just rest awhile. I don't need to be to work until ten," he said softly.

Tucker nodded and didn't move, his breathing evening out once again. Gerome loved that Tucker just went back to sleep. At least he was able to watch him this time.

A knocking reached Gerome's ears. He listened again but didn't hear anything. He had settled back in the bed when the knock sounded again, soft but definitely there.

Gerome got out of bed, pulled on his robe, and went into the other room. This time sniffling caught his hearing, and he went to the door and opened it slowly, finding Joshie outside the door, tears running down his cheeks, the Matchbox car clutched in his hand.

"What are you doing out here?' Gerome asked, lifting Joshie into his arms. "Are you hungry? Where's your mommy?"

"Sleeping and she won't wake up. I shaked her and everything." He wrapped his arms around Gerome's neck, and Gerome carried Joshie inside to the bedroom.

"Tucker, it's Cheryl. Joshie is scared," he said.

Tucker lifted himself out of the bed as Gerome left him to dress quickly. "What's wrong?" Tucker asked, disheveled and running his fingers through his hair, jeans hanging on his narrow hips.

"Mommy won't wake up," Joshie said, still hugging Gerome tightly. He was clearly very scared and confused.

Tucker sprang into action, grabbed his shirt, and raced out of the apartment. Gerome followed and went into the other apartment as Tucker entered her room.

"Cheryl," Tucker said loudly. "What happened?" he asked more softly as Gerome stood outside the door.

"I'm okay," Cheryl answered softly. Gerome put Joshie down, and he ran into the room. "I guess I was just really tired." She hugged Joshie, and Gerome and Tucker left the room so the two of them could be alone.

"Is she ill again?" Gerome asked.

"I don't know. She woke up right away but seemed kind of flushed. I'll let her calm Joshie down and then talk to her." Tucker hugged him, resting his head on Gerome's shoulder. "Thanks for reacting so quickly. I don't know what's going on. It could be that Joshie just got scared."

That seemed like a plausible explanation. "True," Gerome said and looked down, realizing he was still only dressed in a robe. "I need to finish getting ready for work." He leaned down to kiss Tucker. "I'll see you later."

Tucker slid his hand around the back of Gerome's neck, drawing him into a deeper kiss that Gerome felt to his toes.

"Kissing…." Joshie giggled and raced by, still in his pj's. Tucker and Gerome shared a smile, and Gerome returned to his apartment.

THE STORE was slow, and Gerome spent much of the day sitting behind the counter with very little to do. He tried to think about work, but Tucker kept coming to mind.

"How is it going?" Terrance asked as he charged through the front door. "Looks like someone had a really good night." He snickered and leaned over the counter. "You have that well-fucked look."

"Ass," Gerome countered, but he didn't deny it. "I saw another drop last night. Tucker and I got to the bridge, and I think I got the name of one of the boats involved, *Flying Rage*." He spoke softly, even though there was no one in the store. "We have to do something."

"Damned right we do," Terrance said, growing serious. "I saw Winters outside the hardware store."

Gerome tensed. "Shit…."

"Yeah. He didn't see me and didn't stick around, but there are guys from Detroit here on the key. What the fuck do we do? If we tell Elizabeth, we get moved." And that was the last thing Gerome wanted right now. The three of them, along with Daniel and Coby, would just disappear, and Tucker would have no idea. "We gotta get rid of these guys without being seen."

"Any ideas?" Gerome asked.

"Find out where *Flying Rage* is moored and then maybe we can check it out. If it's is involved, then we sink the fucker. Take out their assets." Terrance grinned. "Make them think that doing business here isn't as easy as they thought it would be." This sort of thing was right up Terrance's alley.

"Okay. Do it. We can't be seen, though, and there is no way they can know we're here," Gerome said. "But we gotta scare the shit out of these guys."

Terrance grinned, his eyes shining. "Don't you worry. I think it's time that we take out everyone involved, just in case. Leave it to me." He patted the counter twice and left the shop.

Gerome wondered exactly what Terrance was going to do and figured it was probably best if he didn't know. Terrance was many things—loyal, tenacious, stubborn—and he could be ruthless as all hell.

Gerome meant to ask if Terrance needed to work, but apparently he was on a tear. He sighed and picked up the phone to tell Richard that he needed to talk with him, face-to-face, as soon as possible.

"I'll stop by on my way to work."

Gerome agreed and then hung up. Not that he wanted to stop Terrance. These were people who most definitely needed to get the message to get the hell away, and Terrance was damned good at what he did. Gerome only hoped that whatever Terrance had planned didn't start a fire that none of them could possibly put out.

An hour later Richard hurried inside and checked that they were alone. "What is Terrance up to?"

"He saw some guys from Detroit. Things are getting pretty hot around here right now. Terrance is going to send them a go-away message, but I thought you had better know to be on the watch and damned careful."

Richard growled. "What is he going to do?"

"A little asset removal. Take out what they're using and then make sure there's a trail back to the people we need out of the picture. The usual Terrance special." Gerome was deadly serious.

"Is that wise?" Richard asked.

"What are we going to do, sit here and let these assholes take away what we have? You, Coby, and Daniel ripped away from what you have here? I would never see Tucker again, and we would just be gone. He would be back out on the streets, as would Joshie and Cheryl." Fucking hell, when did they get to be the caretakers of the world? He had no idea, but Gerome had never turned his back on his family, and that now included the people they all cared about. "Any other ideas?"

Richard shrugged. "So, what's the plan?"

"He's going to find the boat we saw last night." Gerome explained the evening's activities. "I asked that he verify that the boat was being used and then sink it and everything on it. Same with Bobby Ramone's boat. Take them to the bottom, deny them resources, send a message to go away. Then call the police and tip them off." Gerome smiled. "They'll investigate suspicious fires, so if they find something illegal, then the heat is on."

"Just like the old days," Richard quipped as the front door opened to a pair of older ladies. He excused himself and left the store so Gerome could help the customers. At least it gave him something to do.

GEROME CLOSED the store, tuning the sound system to a local radio station for something other than the easy-listening Muzak that rang through his head all day long. His phone rang, and he snatched it off the counter, placing it under his chin as he counted the money.

"Gerome…." Terrance sounded pleased. "The boat you told me about was loaded. The assholes were lazy enough that they hadn't moved the product off yet. I found them still in bed, high as kites."

"What did you do?" Gerome asked.

"Set the fire near the engine and then jumped off the boat as it went up, yelling and calling out to rouse them. The two of them stumbled off the boat, coughing. Then the fuel caught fire and the damned boat exploded, taking all the product right along with it. I melted into the crowd and then disappeared before the police got there."

"What are they going to find?" Gerome asked, pleased as hell.

"No doubt what these guys were up to. I can guarantee that with coke packs floating in the water, this is going to be a shit show for them." Terrance was almost gleeful. "I'll talk to you in a little while. I have one more job to do." He hung up, and Gerome put the phone in his pocket. Things were working out well, at least so far. Gerome finished up his tasks, locked the store, and took the deposit to the bank before heading over to the Driftwood to relay the information he had to Richard. He figured he could have a drink and wait for Terrance to call again.

Gerome sat at the bar, watching the people there. Richard was bartending and kept the beer coming. Not that Gerome was drinking a lot. He was too nervous. It had been two hours since he'd heard from Terrance, and he was getting concerned.

"He can take care of himself," Richard said as he passed, setting a BLT with fries in front of him.

"I know. But I'm still worried. What if something happened and he was caught or worse…?" Gerome tried not to be a mother hen, but he worried about his friend. He had expected Terrance to contact him an hour ago. Not that he was going to be able to go out looking for him. That might draw more attention. So he ate his dinner and half watched the door.

Gerome had finished eating and had downed his fourth beer when Terrance finally slunk into the restaurant, taking the seat next to him. "What happened to you?" Terrance looked like he'd been rolled in dirt and all of it had stuck.

"Mission accomplished" was all he said. "Now, please get me a beer." His right hand shook a little, and Gerome leaned closer.

"Mr. Gerome!" Gerome turned as Tucker and Joshie hurried inside, with Joshie running up to his stool. Gerome helped him onto the one next to him.

"Where did you come from?" Gerome asked.

"We should get a table so Richard and Alan don't lose their license," Tucker said, and they shifted to one of the empty tables.

Joshie climbed into the chair next to Terrance and scrunched his nose. "He smells funny," Joshie stage-whispered.

"It's not nice to say things like that," Tucker told Joshie. "He was working really hard today and got dirty. Sometimes you don't smell so nice, like when you played in those puddles a while ago." Tucker grinned. "He smelled like a fish cannery."

"I know. I got yucky, and I have to shower when I get home. But I'm really hungry." Terrance seemed to take it in stride, which was good. Though Gerome was more than curious about what actually happened, he was going to have to wait until they were alone.

"Me too," Joshie said. "Want french fries and fishies, please." He was all ready to eat. Gerome thought it adorable.

"Where's Cheryl?" Gerome asked Tucker.

"She had a sandwich and then went to bed." Tucker drummed his fingers on the table. "She says she's fine, but I'm not so sure. I would have expected her to be tired after being ill, but it's been a while now, and she's still worn out." He smiled at Andi and placed an order for himself and Joshie. Terrance ordered his beer and a mountain of food. Gerome just got a soft drink and sat back. He liked that everyone was here, and when Richard joined them for a little while, they had what seemed like a weird kind of family dinner. Daniel and Coby were all that was missing.

GEROME TOOK Tucker and Joshie home once they had finished their dinners, leaving Tucker to look after the little boy and to check on Cheryl. Terrance went to his place to clean up, but Gerome had little doubt that he would stop back down. He got out the beer, and sure enough Terrance sauntered in barefooted, grabbed a beer, and flopped down on the sofa. "God, you have no idea."

Gerome grabbed one as well and sat across from him. "What happened?"

"The second place was going well, but then I heard voices and had to rush. A group of people got on the boat, and I ended up hiding in the head, ready to take out anyone who found me." Gerome got a vision of

Terrance jammed into one of those tiny spaces. Boat bathrooms weren't known for their size.

"Finally the smoke started coming from the back, and they hurried off the boat, but I was stuck. It was either break my cover or go down with the burning piece of junk. I ended up climbing out of the damned cabin. There was so much smoke I could hardly breathe, and I managed to jump to the boat next door. I could barely see a damned thing, but I managed to get to the next boat and then off and onto the pier. I had to hide behind one of those damned pier boxes until it got dark enough, and then I climbed a fucking fence to get off the far end of the pier and onto dry land. I about kissed the ground and hurried out of there." He gulped his beer. "I hid in the brush until I could get to the car, and finally made it to the restaurant."

"And no one saw you?" Gerome asked.

"You're damned right. With all that smoke, no one was going to see shit. The last I saw, that boat had sunk in place and was one hell of a mess."

"Where did you start the fire?" Gerome asked.

"Off the battery. The wires were in bad shape, so I made them worse and added a little help. It took longer because the damned idiots didn't turn on any lights right away. Once they did, it went up like I hoped." He leaned forward, tapping Gerome's bottle with his own. "Those assets are out of commission, and their shipment is gone. If the money was also paid, then that's gone too. These guys should be hurting big-time." He grinned. "I'd love to hear the panic that's going on about now." Damn, Terrance practically cackled after that. "Whoever their supplier is isn't going to be happy, and the police are going to investigate, so those guys aren't going to get off scot-free. This should scare the shit out of anyone dealing with these yahoos." He grinned and finished his beer, the smile fading from his lips. "I'm getting too old for this shit."

"Don't give me that crap," Gerome teased back. "You love stuff like this… always have."

"Yeah," Terrance retorted without heat or excitement. "So what do we do next? They have to have other assets in the area. There's no way they could be operating out of just those two boats."

"Probably, but I don't know what the other assets are, and we can let the police track those down. We turned up the heat on them a lot, and hopefully the fire is going to send the rats scurrying to a safer place." He finished his beer and set the bottle on the coffee table.

A knock pulled his attention, and Gerome got up to open the door to Tucker, letting him in and handing him a beer. "What's going on?"

"Just shooting the shit. How are Cheryl and Joshie?"

"They were playing together when I left, and she seems like her old self." He sat next to Terrance, and Gerome wished there was room for Tucker next to him. Whenever they were in the same room, Gerome had this urge to touch him. Hell, right now, he wanted to tug Tucker into his arms, soak up his warmth, and feel the energy that rolled off him.

"I think I'll be going home," Terrance said as he pushed himself up off the sofa. "Three is obviously one too many in this little gathering." He set the bottle on the counter as he left and closed the door behind him.

"Does he hate me or something?" Tucker asked.

"I doubt it. Terrance is just touchy right now." Gerome really wished he knew the fuck why. "I think he's feeling a little alone or something. Terrance has always been a little thin-skinned." The more he thought about it, the more Gerome thought it could be the loss of his mother. Her death had hit all three of them pretty hard. Of all the people and parts of his former life, she was what he missed most. Granted, she had passed away, and maybe that only made it harder, because while they had broken the rules to call her before she died, it was still hard to know that none of them had been able to say a true goodbye to her. They hadn't been able to attend the funeral and had had to mourn silently in order to keep their cover intact.

Gerome had come out of the closet a long time ago. But living this life in witness protection felt like going back into the closet in some ways. They all lived a double life filled with secrets and obfuscations, even when dealing with the people closest to them. He couldn't tell Tucker some of the most basic things about himself, and that meant about the loss of one of the people who was kind and cared for him. Keeping secrets was part of his life, but sometimes he wished his life didn't feel like one big secret.

"I don't know about that. Terrance doesn't seem to me to be the kind of guy who's touchy. He's more the kind to be straightforward and just tell it like it is." Tucker took a sip from his bottle. "Joshie certainly isn't scared of him in the least."

Gerome couldn't help smiling. "Yeah. He certainly isn't, telling Terrance that he smelled yucky." An image of Joshie's expression flashed in his mind.

"I always thought that it was hard to fool kids and dogs. They read a person's soul. If you're good, then they know it and want to be near you." Tucker placed his bottle on the coffee table, and Gerome came to sit next to him on the sofa.

"Like this?" Gerome asked.

"Yeah. Except I'm not a dog or a kid," Tucker whispered breathily, his body tensing a little as Gerome drew closer, cheeks growing red.

"No. But I think you have good instincts." Gerome slowly closed the distance between them. "I think you know whether a person is good or not." He held himself a few inches away, holding gazes with Tucker.

"I'm not so sure of that," Tucker said. "If I'm honest, you confound me a little." He swallowed, and Gerome's gaze went to the muscles in his throat. Damn, he wanted to lick that spot just for the soft moan he might get as a reward. "Sometimes I wonder if you're good or bad. I see both in your eyes sometimes." Tucker didn't look away.

"Maybe you're drawn to the bad side just a touch." There was no use denying what Tucker said. It was true. Gerome could be bad. He had been that way for years, and he had done things he wished he could forget. "You came along with me, remember? You insisted." He nudged closer, gliding his fingers along Tucker's jaw, the muscles trembling under his touch.

"Yeah, I did." He didn't lower his gaze, and Gerome basked in his gorgeous cerulean eyes. He could look into them forever, fall into their depths and never find his way out again. That thought would have scared the shit out of him a little while ago, but now it was comforting. There was something soothing in staying right where he was, in this moment… with Tucker. "But you're the leader." His lips curled upward, little lines forming near the edges of his eyes.

"So you liking to walk a little on the bad side is my fault?" Gerome cocked his eyebrows, loving how Tucker's eyes darkened slightly.

"Yeah, of course it is," Tucker countered, and Gerome closed the distance between them. He couldn't argue with the truth, and why even try? "You're the one who led me astray, and you know it."

Gerome was about to protest when Tucker cut him off by sliding his fingers around the back of his neck, tugging him closer until their lips met. After that, Gerome didn't feel like talking.

He let Tucker control the kiss because, hell, Tucker knew how to kiss, his tongue exploring, lips tugging slightly. Gerome moaned softly, loving this time when it was just the two of them.

Tucker shifted without breaking the kiss, climbing on top of the sofa, straddling Gerome's legs. Gerome held Tucker closer, his hands roaming down his back, sliding over his firm butt. Damn, there was so much of Tucker to feel and explore. Even though he had had the chance to do it before, this felt like the first time all over again.

"What is it?" Tucker asked, and Gerome realized he'd gone completely still.

"Nothing," he answered quickly, maybe too fast. But it hit him that he wanted to explore Tucker again and again. Gerome wanted to have Tucker in his arms every night and to wake up next to him each morning. God, Gerome would rather face down half the damned Garvic family than admit that, somehow, Tucker had worked his way into his heart and now held it in his hands. The thing was he didn't even realize it. Gerome tightened his hold, burying his face against Tucker's chest, inhaling deeply.

"It's definitely something," Tucker pressed, gently touching his chin.

Gerome lifted his gaze. "I hate being…." He found it hard to say the words.

Tucker's gaze softened as he swallowed. "We all do. No one likes being at the mercy of things we can't control, and it's natural to be a little afraid of the things that are new to us." Tucker had actually said exactly what he was feeling. Gerome didn't like admitting it, but it was true.

"How do you know that?" It was even more frightening that Tucker not only understood, but was able to anticipate his feelings.

"It's human nature." Tucker shrugged. "New things are frightening, and I was assuming that this… what's happening between us… is just as new for you as it is for me. Maybe that was wrong." His voice grew more tentative.

Gerome shook his head. "You aren't wrong. It's just frightening to have someone else in my head… in a way."

Now Tucker rolled his eyes and laughed. "It isn't your head." He placed his hand on Gerome's chest. "It's right here. This sort of connection doesn't happen in your head." Tucker looked at him as though he were completely ridiculous. "It's your heart that speaks to me." He cupped Gerome's cheeks in his soft, warm hands. "I know you like to cover things up, but your heart comes through no matter what. And you gave us a place to live and helped us with jobs… all of that tells just what's in your heart."

"That was just…."

Tucker smirked. "Would Terrance have done that? Would Richard? Or that Bobby Ramone guy?" He cocked his light brown eyebrows. "No, they wouldn't. Richard is a good guy, and Terrance… but those were things that you did. Nobody else—you." Tucker's gaze bored deep into him, and for a second he wondered if Tucker could see clear to his soul, which was frightening as hell. He had wondered what was written there. Gerome closed his eyes in order to block out Tucker's penetrative gaze.

Gerome knew his soul was not squeaky clean. The things he'd done in the past had to have left a mark, even if it was only on the inside, where it wasn't readily apparent. What would Tucker think if he discovered his past? Gerome didn't want to think about it.

"I don't know what anyone else would do, and if I'm honest with you, I don't even know why I did the things I did myself." He kept going back to Terrance's mother, one of the toughest and kindest souls he probably would ever meet in his life. Maybe that small woman with the spirit as big as all outdoors left a deeper impression than he even wanted to admit to himself.

Tucker leaned closer, his lips coming close enough to Gerome's ear that he could feel his breath. "That's because sometimes our brains and our heart are on different wavelengths. The heart is stronger, and it guides you in ways that you may not understand. Logic is good, but it doesn't have all the answers." He sat up. "What are you so afraid of? That someone might know that you aren't the biggest badass on earth? Because, dude, I think Terrance has you beat by a mile on that one."

"You're probably right." Gerome could hardly believe he had Tucker across his legs and in his arms, so damned close, and they were talking about their feelings. He never did that. Usually if a guy was this close to him, there was fucking involved, and here the two of them were, talking about their feelings and shit like that. The worst thing was that it made him feel better and tended to calm some of the anxiety from traveling into the unknown because maybe Tucker knew what was happening. "Maybe we should…." He chuckled. "Hell, I don't fucking know what…."

Tucker once again drew closer, his gaze smoldering, sending a zing racing through Gerome. This he understood, and as he took Tucker's lips in a searing kiss, possessing his mouth, he could forget the confusion and uncertainty as his feet once again hit solid, familiar ground. His heart knew what it wanted, and so did his body and head. For once they were in complete agreement, and the conflict inside that he wasn't sure how to manage melted away. "You know, I was going to say that we could just get to the fucking and stop analyzing everything, but I think you get that idea loud and clear." He kissed him again, and Gerome leaned forward, flexing his legs to get to his feet. Tucker held tighter, wrapping his legs around his waist as Gerome carried him to the bedroom.

"OH GOD!" Tucker shouted an hour or so later, sending them both tumbling into a mind-numbing release that Gerome wished could go on and on.

His heart pounding in his ears, Gerome settled on the bed, gasping for air and wishing he had the stamina to continue longer. But damn… just damn.

Tucker ran his hand over Gerome's chest, tweaking a nipple and settling right next to him. "I don't think I'll be able to move for the rest of the night."

Gerome only had the energy to hum his agreement, and he closed his eyes, letting fatigue take over. It was all he was able to do.

"Gerome," Tucker said just as he started to nod off.

"Huh?" he whispered as Tucker got out of bed and went to the bathroom. "Where are you going?"

"There's someone at the door," Tucker said, returning to the room. "I think it's Joshie."

Gerome climbed out of bed and tugged on his jeans, then pulled on a T-shirt as the knocking came again. This time he recognized it and hurried out. Joshie stood outside, looking lost. "Where's your mommy?"

"Sleeping," Joshie said and put his finger to his lips. Gerome lifted him into his arms and took him inside. "Mommy said to be quiet. Shhhh…."

Gerome shared a look with Tucker, who went across the hall and raced back. "Call an ambulance," he said softly.

Gerome dialed 911, trying to stay calm so he didn't panic Joshie. Tucker went back into the other apartment as Gerome relayed the information requested. He hung on the line and whispered for Joshie to go get his trucks. Gerome took Joshie to his apartment and closed the door, settling him on the floor to play. Then he checked with Tucker.

"What's going on?"

"She's alive but barely breathing, and I can't wake her. I'll handle the ambulance people when they arrive. Keep Joshie inside and out of sight. We can take care of him until Cheryl comes home."

Gerome read the fear in Tucker's eyes, and Gerome understood it immediately. He handed Tucker the phone to speak with the emergency personnel as sirens drew closer; then he closed the door and turned on the radio to cover as much noise from outside as possible.

For the first time, he wished he had a house phone. He wanted to call the guys and let them know what was happening, but he needed to stay here.

A knock sent him hurrying to the door, and Tucker handed him the phone. "They're taking her in," he said softly.

"But what happened?" Gerome asked.

Tucker shrugged, looking completely devastated. "I don't know. But she stopped breathing and they started her up again. They're taking her to St. Michael's, but I can't go, and I need to stay here with Joshie."

"Did they ask about him?" Gerome asked.

"I said he was with a friend and that I was her partner, so they didn't question me further." He shifted from foot to foot. "I don't know what to do."

"Go with her." Gerome handed Tucker his change bowl and then paused. "Do you still have the phone I gave you?"

Tucker nodded.

"Let me get you numbers." He hurriedly wrote down phone numbers and handed the piece of paper to Tucker. "I'll stay here with Joshie and make sure he's taken care of. Just call when you know something." He hugged Tucker tightly, not wanting to let him go, but the ambulance was getting ready to go, so he watched Tucker leave and then closed the door and sent messages to the guys that he needed their help.

It grew quiet outside the door, and Joshie continued playing until knocks were followed by the guys entering, Daniel and Coby flooding into the apartment. Coby and Joshie immediately set to playing, and Gerome took the others to the kitchen.

"What happened?" Daniel asked, and Gerome gave all of them a rundown.

"What if something happens to her?" Richard asked.

All Gerome could do was shrug. He had no idea. "I have to ask Tucker if he and Cheryl made any sort of arrangements. I doubt it, though." He turned his attention to where the little boy played happily on the floor, oblivious to the upheaval in his life that was waiting just around the corner.

"You know that as soon as something happens, Child Services will be here so fast it will make your head spin," Daniel said softly and then sighed.

"Yeah, great. Joshie can enter the system so he can have the same damned kind of childhood that we had," Richard whispered.

Gerome found himself nodding. Even Terrance seemed pained, and he turned to Joshie with a frown.

"No kid should have to go through that," Terrance added.

Gerome's phone vibrated, and he pulled it out of his pocket. "Tucker?" he asked quietly at the familiar number.

"Yeah, it's me. She's alive, but in a coma." His voice broke. "They don't seem to know if she's going to wake up. Right now they said that they're running tests, but I can't get any additional information because I'm not listed on a privacy sheet. I'm sitting here and waiting, but I don't know if I'll ever learn anything at all. They're hiding behind a wall of privacy, and I can't get past it."

"Do you want one of us to come get you?" Gerome asked.

"I don't know what I can do here. They won't let me see her because I'm not family, and she's being transferred to ICU. I guess if someone can come get me, I can try to return in the morning. I left your phone number in case something happens, and I can hope they'll call." He seemed bereft and lost.

"I'm on my way," Terrance said. He grabbed his keys and headed out. Gerome made sure he knew where to go, and then he was gone.

Gerome explained what was happening to Tucker. "Just come to my place. We'll figure things out once you get here." He ended the call and quietly brought everyone else up to date.

"That doesn't sound good," Daniel said.

Gerome had to agree, but he wasn't sure what the hell to do.

Daniel went to see to the boys, and Gerome pulled out some beer and chips and placed them on the counter. He also got some water and small bowls so the boys could have a snack before bed.

"What the hell are we going to do? If anything happens to her, his world will be ripped away." They both knew damned well what that felt like.

"Do we know who Joshie's father is?" Richard asked. "Are there any sort of papers at all?"

Gerome shrugged. "I think Cheryl had a few things that she brought with her. They could be in the car. I don't know. Why?"

Richard shrugged. "We'll see if we can find them, I guess. Right now, we don't need to borrow trouble. We can wait to see what happens." He had that look that told Gerome that Richard was churning something in that head of his. But he wouldn't be ready to talk about it until he had mulled it over, and Richard wasn't going to be pushed.

"Do you boys want some chips?" Gerome asked, and they hurried over, each taking a bowl before racing back to their cars. It was like they had endless energy, until the food was gone and the water glasses were empty. Coby climbed on the sofa, and Daniel put on a movie. Both boys were asleep in less than twenty minutes.

"Any ideas?" Daniel asked, looking at Richard. "We could take him," Daniel suggested. "He and Coby get along really well, and we already have a child. I'm sure we could get some support if we needed it."

Richard didn't seem as enthusiastic. "There is another option, I think."

"So you do have an idea?" Daniel asked. He could worm anything out of Richard. Ever since the two of them got together, Daniel had been able to get Richard to do just about anything. Richard definitely hated to disappoint Daniel.

"Just don't push it right now. Let me mull it over," he said, moving closer. "I hate to disturb those two, but we need to get Coby home and off to bed. You have work to do, and I need to check in with Alan."

"We'll stay until Tucker and Terrance get back, and then we can leave," Daniel said. He turned off the television, lowering the lights around where the boys slept.

Gerome found it hard not to watch Joshie sleep. He was so adorable, innocent, and the one who was most likely to be hurt the most in all of this. "I can't let anything happen to him. I just can't." Bile rose in the back of his throat, and he swallowed it down. "No kid should go through what we did."

"I agree," Richard whispered.

They sat quietly, Gerome half dozing until footsteps sounded outside the door. Gerome let Tucker and Terrance inside.

"Any news?" Gerome asked. Tucker shook his head. "Go and put Joshie to bed. Daniel and Richard are going to take Coby home, and I'll come over once he's settled and we can talk."

"Okay." Tucker rubbed his puffy eyes and gently lifted Joshie into his arms, making soothing sounds as he left.

Gerome hugged both Richard and Daniel, wondering what he was going to do.

"One step at a time," Daniel whispered to him during their hug before gathering Coby into his arms and carrying him out as well. Richard gathered Coby's toys and quietly said goodbye.

Gerome shut the door and leaned against it, wondering what the hell had happened to his life and why he didn't feel like running for the hills. Instead, he stayed still, listened, and then went over to check on Tucker and Joshie. He couldn't just sit in his apartment and do nothing.

Once inside, he quietly began picking up. The place wasn't dirty or anything, just messy because a five-year-old lived there. He took care of the dishes and folded the blankets strewn around the sofa. By the time Tucker emerged from the bedroom, Gerome had everything under control, and he joined Tucker on the awful sofa.

"I gave them your number…." Tucker stared straight ahead.

"You said. There hasn't been anything, so that's good. Do you have any idea what happened?" Gerome put an arm around Tucker, holding him close.

"She was having a real hard time breathing when I found her. I didn't know what to do. She kept gasping like she was being strangled or something. By the time the ambulance got here, she had stopped breathing. They put a tube in and brought her back, but she wasn't breathing for a while. I don't know what that means."

Gerome did. Lack of oxygen to the brain. He didn't say anything more because speculation was less than helpful at the moment.

"If something happens to her, what are we going to do?" Tucker asked, wiping his eyes and then turning toward Gerome, burying his face against his chest.

"I don't know. Did she have any papers or things like that? Birth certificate? Did she give you any indication of what she might want?" Gerome asked.

Tucker wiped his eyes and sniffed. "She told me more than once that she wished I was Joshie's father, but I doubt she ever made a will or anything or even wrote it down. It was just something she said a few times."

"We need to look in the car and see if there is anything in there. Then we'll have to figure things out once we see what the situation is."

Tucker nodded. "If something happens to her, they're going to take Joshie away, I know it, and then what will happen to him?" He shook, and Gerome held him tightly, wishing he had some answers to give him.

GEROME STAYED with Tucker well into the night. He fell asleep on the sofa, and Gerome covered him with a blanket, leaning back and eventually falling asleep himself. Dawn had just broken and light was coming in the apartment windows when his phone vibrated on the table. He picked it up quickly as Tucker sprang awake. Gerome didn't recognize the local number, but he answered it.

"This is Angela Wilson with patient advocacy at St. Michael's. We have a request to notify this number on any developments regarding Cheryl Henning."

Gerome swallowed. "Yes. Is she okay? We're the friends of hers who called emergency services."

"Are you her next of kin?" Angela asked, and Gerome knew in his heart the news he was about to be given.

"Tucker and I are as close to family as she has at the moment," Gerome explained. He felt Tucker tense next to him. "As far as we are aware, she doesn't have any direct family." Okay, that was a lie, but he wasn't going to bring Joshie into this. If the hospital was aware of him, they would get involved in Joshie's welfare, and that was a path that none of them were ready for.

"I see." She hesitated. "I'm sorry, but Cheryl hasn't regained consciousness, and her condition remains critical. I don't have any other information I can share right now."

"I see." He met Tucker's gaze and saw some of the light go out of his eyes. "Thank you for calling. We appreciate it very much." He hung up the call and enfolded Tucker in his arms. Gerome knew he'd have to say the words eventually, but right now all he wanted to do was comfort Tucker and somehow get ready to try to reassure a little boy whose mom was so sick and the only family he had.

"I'm okay," Tucker said eventually. "And she will be. She has to."

"Go out to the car and quietly go through it. See if there is anything in there as far as papers, birth certificates, anything you can find."

"Why?"

"Just do it, right now. Okay?" he asked gently, but with a sense of urgency. As soon as Tucker was gone, he made another call and told Richard that he needed him and Daniel right away.

"It's six in the morning," Richard growled.

"Cheryl is really ill and hasn't come around… and I have an idea. You need to get yourselves over here now. Please," he added for good measure and then ended the call. He was wired and knew that they needed to do this quickly if it was going to work.

"I found this stuff in the glove box," Tucker said when he came back in, handing Gerome an envelope.

Gerome spread out the papers on the table and went through them. Thankfully he found birth certificates for both Cheryl and Joshua. Joshie's papers listed the father as unknown. "What are we going to do? Joshie is going to be up soon."

"I need you to stay here with him. I have some things I need to do at my place. Just stay, feed him breakfast, and tell him nothing for now." He held Tucker's gaze.

"Okay. But what's going to happen to him? Will they take him away if she doesn't recover?" Tucker asked, his voice breaking.

"Do you want them to?" Gerome asked.

Tucker's eyes filled with horror. "Of course not. How can you think that?" It was clear that Tucker's heart was aching for Joshie.

Gerome nodded. "So, if you could be Joshie's guardian…?" he prompted. "Don't ask any more questions, but just answer me. You need to make a decision right away."

"But I'm not his parent," Tucker added, near tears, his hand shaking.

Gerome held Tucker's gaze, as serious as a heart attack. "Yes. But would you care for him if he needed it? Can you make that commitment, right now?" Gerome waited for hesitation of any kind.

"Yes," Tucker answered in an instant. He had no doubt.

"Then stay here with him, say nothing, and for God's sake do not ever ask any questions." Gerome kissed him and left the apartment, hoping to hell he was doing the right thing… for all of them.

Chapter 10

TUCKER WONDERED what the heck had just happened. Suddenly Gerome had disappeared after asking him if he wanted to be Joshie's dad. Cheryl was really sick, and Joshie was frightened all to heck. He shook and stayed right where he was because the thought of getting to his feet made him ill. His entire life had just changed. Somehow he had to make sure that Joshie was going to be okay.

He took a deep breath and tried to clear his head. Cheryl was really sick, and… what could he do? How could he…? Not that it mattered. He wasn't going to let Joshie go into a foster home if he could help it. Tucker tried to think of ways that he could keep Joshie. Maybe he could write a letter to say that Cheryl wanted him to have Joshie, somehow make it look like she signed it. Not that he could do such a thing, but now....

"Tucker," Joshie said in the bedroom doorway, wiping his eyes, wearing the blue pajamas that Daniel had brought over for him. "Where's Mommy?" He hurried over and climbed on the sofa, whimpering a little.

Tucker let Joshie curl into him. "It's going to be okay," he lied through his teeth. Tucker definitely did not see how anything was ever going to be all right again, but he had to do something. Telling Joshie about his mom was not something he was looking forward to. How did you tell a five-year-old that his mother was so sick that she could die and leave him alone in the world? Tucker wiped his eyes and tried to stop his head from spinning.

"Are you hungry?" Tucker asked.

Joshie nodded, and Tucker got up to make a little breakfast. At least it gave him something to do for right now and a chance to try to think things through.

Tucker turned the television to cartoons and let Joshie watch as he made some toast and eggs. He couldn't help wondering what Gerome was up to. The questions he'd asked left Tucker wondering yet again just who Gerome was. He'd said he wasn't a police officer, and yet he knew all this stuff. There were definitely things about him that Tucker didn't know, and he was getting more and more curious about what Gerome was hiding.

Tucker fixed Joshie's plate and brought it over to him. Joshie slid onto the floor, slipping his legs under the coffee table, and Tucker handed him a fork. Joshie dug in the way he always did, devouring his food like someone was going to take it away from him.

"I'll bring you some milk, and then I need to check on Mr. Gerome."

"And Mommy," Joshie added, still eating. "Don't forget to find Mommy." Like she was lost or something.

Tucker swallowed hard and stepped out, going to the door across the way.

"You have to tell him," someone said. "Tucker deserves to know and make his own decision. You can't just do this." It was Daniel.

Tucker stepped away and went back inside, silently shutting the door, wondering what the hell secrets they all had been keeping. God, he felt like an idiot. Tucker had trusted Gerome and the guys, and they had helped him. He knew Gerome wasn't telling him something, and the way the guys clammed up before.... They were all in on something big....

They were doing something that involved him, though apparently he didn't get a choice as far as the others were concerned. Only Daniel was standing up for him, not Gerome. Whatever the hell was going on, he deserved to be the one to make decisions about himself, and Gerome should have been the one standing up for him. Tucker didn't like this at all. Cheryl was sick, and Gerome and his friends were making decisions for him.

Tucker was beginning to think that he should get the hell out of here. But where the hell was he going to go? He couldn't leave Cheryl and Joshie to the wolves. He didn't have any right to take Joshie anywhere. At least he would be the one making the decisions for himself again, as opposed to Gerome and his friends deciding things for him.

While Joshie ate, Tucker started getting his stuff into his bag. Once he was done, he went into the bedroom and got the old plastic tubs Cheryl had used to pack Joshie's and her things, folded Joshie's clothes, and started filling them. He left Cheryl's things for now—they weren't going to need them anyway, and they could live in the tent once again and he could determine his own life.

"Joshie, when you're done eating, you should get dressed," Tucker said gently, trying not to panic as the impact of everything seemed to descend around him. He was actually thinking of taking Joshie away and.... God, what was he doing?

Tucker sat on the edge of Cheryl's bed as tears filled his eyes. She had been his sister and his protector when he'd found himself alone on the streets. Cheryl had fed him when he was starving, and she had watched over him when he had been alone. The thought of losing Cheryl scared him to death, but it was nothing compared to what Joshie was going to feel once Tucker told him how bad things were. Tucker knew what it felt like to lose parents and to be cast adrift, but he had been an adult, or nearly so. Joshie was five and could end up in the same place. Hell, they were all each other had, and Tucker just couldn't cut Joshie loose. The thought of losing him nearly sent him to the bathroom. But somehow he held it together.

"Mr. Terrance!" Joshie squealed with delight, and Tucker shuffled to his feet.

Terrance had Joshie in the air, whirling him around like an airplane to happy laughter.

"Gerome asked me to come over so you could go to his place. He has some things he needs to talk to you about," Terrance said, and Tucker knew his smile was forced. "I'll watch the little dude here."

Tucker hesitated but then nodded. "I'll be back," he told Joshie. He crossed the hall, knocked, and went inside.

Richard, Daniel, and Gerome sat on the sofa, all looking at him. Tucker felt like he was walking into an inquisition. To his surprise, it was Daniel who got up to meet him, shooting a cold look at the other two. "I want to start by saying how sorry I am—we all are—that Cheryl is so sick. She's a kind lady, and there isn't enough of that in this world." He shot another look at the guys. "Mostly there's assholeness and stubborn idiots, but thankfully they see reason eventually." He rolled his eyes and pulled out one of the chairs at the counter, offering Tucker the other one.

"What are you all doing?" Tucker asked.

"Well, it seems that our two friends over there have an idea how to help you and Joshie if something happens. They were just going to do it, but I didn't agree, and since they need my mad computer skills to make this happen, I refused. You need to know the decisions you're making, and then we can go from there." For the first time, Daniel seemed nervous as he slid a piece of paper across the table.

"What's this?"

"Joshie's birth certificate," Daniel answered. "It's from a small town in Georgia, just across the border. You'll notice that the father's name is listed as unknown."

Tucker sighed. "Cheryl always said she refused to tell anyone who Joshie's father was in case he decided to fight for him." He pushed the piece of paper back to Daniel.

Daniel leaned slightly forward. "I have to ask you some questions, and I want you to understand that you can never tell anyone about any of this, ever. This conversation must go to the grave with you, okay?"

Tucker wondered what was so important, but he agreed.

"Okay. So here's our plan. If the state finds out about Joshie—that his mother is in the hospital and can't take care of him—they will make him a ward of the state. And if they find out Cheryl is homeless, she might not get him back. There is no father on the birth certificate, and as far as we can tell, no will or statement of intent." Daniel paused, and Tucker nodded his understanding. "What the guys want me to do is to create a letter, a note, something… to be found among Cheryl's things, that states that it is her intent that if anything happened to her that she wanted you to look after Joshie." Daniel held his gaze. "Is that what you want?"

He nodded. The thought of Joshie going into foster care with strangers scared the shit out of him. He knew how terrible that could be.

"You need to say the words," Daniel said.

"Yes. I'll take care of Joshie as though he were my own child. But Cheryl didn't have anything like that."

Daniel glanced at the others. "Look, I can create a document and pull a signature from one of the others that she had. I'd change it a little so it was unique and then apply it to the document. If something were to happen to Cheryl, then we could use it to prove her intent and help ensure that Joshie would be taken care of. If she recovers…." And Tucker knew that was a long shot. "Then we destroy the document."

"You can do that?" Tucker asked.

"It will stand up to a pretty close examination because I know what I'm doing, and I have an old printer that isn't perfect. I'll print it on that and go from there."

He leaned closer. "You need to understand. If we do that, then getting custody of Joshie will be relatively easy because there will be a statement of the parent's wishes, and the two of you should be able to move forward. This isn't going to be like an official will, but it will help." Daniel once again turned to Richard and Gerome. "You both made your opinions clear, but they don't matter—only Tucker's does." Damn, Tucker definitely didn't want to get on Daniel's bad side.

"I was just going to say that it was up to him," Gerome clarified. "There's no shame in saying no."

"But…." This was a huge decision, one that was going to affect his and Joshie's lives forever, and he was being asked to make it right away.

Gerome came over and put his arms around him, pressing his chest to Tucker's back. "Just breathe. Whatever you decide, none of us is in any position to second-guess you or pass any sort of judgment," he said softly.

Tucker swallowed. "Of course I'll take care of Joshie. There's no doubt about that. What I don't understand is how you guys think you can do all this and what in the hell made you come up with this?" He paused. "Who the hell are all of you? CIA? Government shadow people? Foreign agents? I don't get it. You all know so much about how things work and about these bad guys. Are you all undercover?" He just wanted some answers.

"They are none of that, trust me. But let's take it one step at a time. Okay? Do you want me to make you Joshie's guardian if Cheryl passes away?" Daniel held Tucker's gaze. "You have to say the words."

"Yes. I always wanted to have children. But how am I going to take care of him?" Tucker asked, growing more and more confused.

"You have a job, and from there, you can get an apartment and start to rebuild your life," Gerome told him. "You don't have to do this alone."

Tucker nodded and tried to concentrate on just one thing. If Daniel could do what he said he could, then Tucker would be listed as Joshie's guardian. They could move forward and Joshie wouldn't be taken away.

"Yeah, do it," Tucker said with more conviction than he really felt.

"Are you sure?" Daniel asked.

"Yes. I'm sure." The thought of doing this alone was daunting, but the idea of letting Joshie go to strangers who didn't love him was terrifying.

"Okay. Give me a few minutes." Daniel grabbed his bag and pulled out a laptop and other equipment that he placed on the counter and got set up.

"All right." He turned on some of the equipment and began typing. It wasn't a long document, and it sounded official. Tucker noticed that Daniel added a few small misspellings and then set up the printer, which took a while to print the document. By the time it was done, it looked old. Then Daniel went back and worked some magic on the signature before adding it. Then he ran it through the copier and crumpled and folded it a number of times to age the cheap paper and make it look worn. Daniel put all the equipment away.

"It's that easy?" Tucker asked as Daniel handed him the document.

"If someone were to look closely, they might discover something, but it isn't likely. Just put the document in the glove compartment of the car and put everything else back. If someone comes, you can hunt for the documents and this will be among them. From there you'll have to handle all the legalities, but the letter should give you standing with the authorities."

Tucker sighed. "So how do you know how to do this?" he persisted.

Daniel shrugged. "Look, sometimes there are times when we shouldn't ask questions." He sat down next to him. "You know that what I did was illegal. But I did it for the best of reasons. Richard and Gerome could tell you how hard it was growing up in foster care, and we didn't want Joshie to have to do that. It's clear to all of us how much you love that little boy."

"But…."

Daniel patted his shoulder. "I think you and Gerome need to have a discussion sometime soon. But this is a conversation that the two of you need to have. If I can offer some advice, though, wait until all of this dies down a little. Joshie is going to need you, and he's going to be very scared. Concentrate on him for the next few days and make sure that he gets what he needs. There will be plenty of time for all the answers to your questions."

Daniel slipped off his chair and sat down next to Richard. Tucker leaned back, and Gerome was right there, his arms encircling him.

"Do you want me to come with you so you can talk to Joshie?" Gerome offered.

Tucker's first instinct was to refuse, but the thought of doing this alone was so daunting. He shrugged, and Gerome pulled away and took his hand, leading him out.

"Thanks, you guys," Tucker said, and then they left.

Terrance and Joshie were still playing, the huge man racing around the floor with Joshie squealing and laughing all during their truck race.

"Is everything all set?" Terrance asked as he got up off the floor.

"Yes," Gerome answered, and then hugged him. It surprised Tucker to see the two huge men hugging each other so tightly. Part of him was actually jealous of the closeness they shared. "Thank you for everything."

"I'll see you later. I was going to order a pizza in a while. You want me to get something for you guys too?" Terrance asked, and Gerome shook his head.

Then Terrance left, and Tucker sat down on the sofa, motioning Joshie over. Nothing he had ever done prepared him for what he was going to have to do.

Gerome sat in the chair across from them, probably to stay close, which Tucker appreciated. But he still had trouble finding the words. "Joshie," he started softly, lifting him onto his lap. "You know your mommy has been sick."

He nodded. "I bring her juice." He struggled to get down, and Tucker held him a little tighter.

"She wasn't that kind of sick. Your mama, she's still in the hospital, and she's really sick." Tucker nearly broke down as those words crossed his lips. "And I don't know when she'll be coming back."

Joshie stared at him and then began to cry. "I want Mommy." Joshie's wails ate at the last of Tucker's control, and he cried right along with him, holding Joshie to his chest. He had no idea what more to say.

Gerome shifted to sit next to him and held Tucker's hand in his.

"I want Mommy."

"I know you do," Tucker said. "But she can't come back right now." There was nothing more to be said. Tucker could only let Joshie cry it out. He had no illusions that this was going to be the only time. They had a very hard road ahead of them as far as hope and recovery were concerned.

"Why?" Joshie asked. "Was she bad?"

Tucker wiped the tears from Joshie's face. "I don't know why, and no, she wasn't bad. Your mommy was good, really good. But she's really sick, and I'm going to take care of you until she gets better." He hugged Joshie some more, and Joshie whimpered softly, holding to Tucker tightly. Tucker wondered what he could do to make this easier on Joshie and realized there was nothing. This was the most difficult kind of situation there was. Tucker could do nothing to make it any easier, other than to be there.

"Do you want something to drink?" Gerome asked.

Tucker nodded, tears still running down his cheeks. Gerome got up and left the two of them alone.

"Your mom is really good. She is kind and thoughtful and loves you very much." He inhaled, even as tears ran down his own cheeks. "I promise to love and take care of you until…." He paused. "Until she gets better." There was nothing he could do except ensure that Joshie was cared for and to pray.

"Can I play with my trucks?" Joshie asked as Gerome handed him a cup with a lid.

Tucker let him get down, his throat too rough to actually talk. Joshie slid onto the floor, drank some of the milk Gerome had gotten for him, then set the cup on the coffee table and began silently running his trucks around the floor.

This was different. There were no truck sounds or laughter, just silence. Tucker almost wished that Joshie would cry some more or get mad. But he supposed everyone dealt with worry in their own way. At five, Joshie might not understand the concepts of potential death and loss. Right now they needed to concentrate on what hope there was.

"I wish I could spare him all of this," Tucker told Gerome softly.

"Know it or not, you spared him one of the worst things that could possibly happen to him. He'll always have you to look out for him and make sure that he grows up in a family and has the best chance in life." He sat down next to Tucker, the both of them watching Joshie.

Joshie hurried over behind his truck and hit the coffee table with his leg. Tucker grabbed him before he could fall, but Joshie burst into tears, calling for his mom, and all Tucker could do was hold him, rocking gently back and forth. The worry for both of them was going to stay just below the surface. He needed to try to keep hope alive.

Tucker held Joshie until he wore himself out and fell asleep. Tucker laid him on the sofa and covered him up, then went into the bedroom and found an old stuffed bear that had pretty much lost its shape. Tucker pressed it into Joshie's arms, and he took it without even waking. "He's going to need all the comfort he can get."

"We'll all be here," Gerome offered and enclosed Tucker in his arms.

"How can you know that?" Tucker asked, even as he leaned back into the embrace, needing it and wanting desperately to know that Gerome was going to be there. "There are so many secrets that you all keep. That isn't the way to raise a child if I have to. I need to know the truth just so I can make my own decisions." He turned in his arms. "You have to either let me choose for myself or walk away. I can't live with lies and cover-ups."

Gerome sighed and his arms slipped away. "I will tell you what you need to know." For the first time, Tucker saw fear in Gerome's gaze. Even when they were breaking into boats and sneaking onto docks, Gerome hadn't been afraid, but now he was. "I don't want to do it now because it would be too much, but I will, I promise, and then you can make your choice." The fear increased, and Tucker understood. Gerome was scared Tucker wouldn't choose him.

Sometimes there are moments in life when things become clear, and maybe this was one of them. Gerome actually paled, and in that moment, Tucker understood Gerome's depth of feeling. Gerome had something to lose, and it scared him just as much as what was happening between them frightened Tucker.

Putting yourself out there for someone else was always difficult, at least for Tucker. He had never had good luck with close relationships. Even his family had been problematic and had rejected him when they knew who he really was. It made it hard to trust people, and now that Cheryl was so sick, the circle of people he was willing to trust had just shrunk. Tucker was aware that Gerome was trying to build trust, but the secrets made it hard for Tucker to do that.

"I need to have something solid to put my feet on," Tucker explained once he'd found the words. "You and your friends have been better to me than my family."

He looked at Joshie, curled on his side, clutching his bear, his face relaxed in sleep. "To all of us."

"I know. It's hard to trust someone when you know they're keeping something from you," Gerome said. "I just can't pile more on you right now." He picked up his phone and made a quick telephone call, ordering some food and arranging delivery. "Joshie should probably be awake by the time it arrives, and he'll be hungry."

The little guy usually was. Joshie was probably going through a growth spurt. "What do I tell him when he asks where his mother is?" Tucker asked.

"Be as honest as you can. She's in the hospital where the doctors and nurses are trying to help her get better," Gerome answered without hesitation. "It's the truth and it's what we hope will happen. That's what we all need to hang on to." Gerome turned away, and Tucker saw him wiping his eyes. "My mother was sick for a long time before she died." Gerome's tone was like he was confessing something.

"Do you have any pictures of her?" Tucker asked.

Gerome nodded. "I have just a few. I keep them packed away in a safe place. They have been with me for a long time, and I couldn't part with them, even after everything that's happened in the intervening years."

"I have some pictures of my family too. I keep them out of sight because I don't want to be reminded of them all the time."

Gerome hugged him tightly, and they stayed quiet, just together. Tucker appreciated how tender and understanding Gerome was being. It was hard to put into words just how reassuring his strength was.

Tucker laid his head on Gerome's shoulder and stayed that way. Having someone to share the burden with was priceless.

"Mommy," Joshie said after a while, his eyes drifting open.

"I'm here," Tucker said.

"I want Mommy," Joshie demanded.

"I know. But Mommy is in the hospital now." He wondered how many times he was going to have to explain the same thing. "But I'm here, and Mr. Gerome ordered a pizza, so we can have it in a few minutes." He gathered a still groggy Joshie into his arms. "Do you need to go potty?"

Joshie nodded and slipped down. "I do it," he said and hurried to the bathroom.

Tucker waited for him to return… and waited…. Then he got up and went to the bathroom door. He knocked and slowly opened the door to find Joshie sitting on the floor, holding his mother's nightgown.

"I be good, I promise, Mommy. You get better." He nodded as he sat looking at the bathtub.

"What are you doing?" Tucker asked.

Joshie looked at him. "Talking to Mommy." He sniffled and then turned back toward the bathtub, waving and saying goodbye. Tucker put out his arms, and Joshie dropped the nightgown and went right to his arms. "Mommy says bye." He put his head on Tucker's shoulder, crying softly. "I don't want her to go."

"Your mommy is sick right now, and we're going to pray for her so she will get better," Tucker said, trying not to make too big a deal of what he had just witnessed. Sometimes he wondered how his little mind worked and the notions he came up with.

The front door opened and closed, and then it did again. "Do you want some pizza?" Tucker asked, and Joshie nodded.

THE REST of the day was hard, with Joshie playing, asking questions, crying some and asking for Cheryl, and then going back to playing. By the time Tucker put him down for the night, he was exhausted beyond belief. "You know, we should get Joshie a bed of his own," Gerome said.

"But where would we put it?" Tucker asked.

"I bet we could rearrange the furniture in the bedroom and create a space for Joshie with a screen. He could have his own bed, and so could you. That way you wouldn't need to sleep on the sofa."

It was a good suggestion, but Tucker didn't have the money for something like that. And more to the point, they only had the apartment for a month or so, and then it would be gone. Even now that he was working, there was little hope that Tucker would be able to afford the place on his own.

"Think about it. He's going to need someone nearby until Cheryl comes back."

"I know. But there's so much unknown right now. I can't really think too far ahead." Tucker agreed that something needed to be done, but that was too many steps ahead. Right now he needed sleep and for his head to be quiet for a while. Not that he thought that was realistically going to happen.

"It's okay." Gerome tugged him into a deep hug and then kissed him. "You get some rest. I'll be just across the hall. I have to work tomorrow, but you two need to take it easy and take the time to figure things out."

"Why do I feel like I'm in a holding pattern?" Tucker was a little confused and growing overwhelmed as a myriad of questions kept coming to him. Childcare, housing, food—everything flooded into his head.

Gerome nodded. "Because you are. We need to make sure that Joshie is okay and hope that Child Services doesn't come looking for him now that Cheryl is hospitalized. What we need is for Cheryl to get better, and we have to keep hoping for that."

"So now I have something else to worry about," Tucker whispered, his shoulders heavy with the burdens being placed on them. "I mean, Bobby Ramone is still out there, I now have Joshie to care for…." Not that he regretted that decision. "I have to worry about him being taken away and how to build a future of some sort."

"I know. It's a lot of change."

"And I have to figure out day care so I can work," Tucker added as his head began to pound.

"I think we can get help until we know more about Cheryl and if she'll improve. Until then, Daniel works from home, and he's agreed that Joshie and Coby can spend the days together with him while you work. At least until we can get him into school. Joshie is old enough for kindergarten in the fall." Gerome shook his head and rolled his eyes.

"What?" Tucker snapped and wished he hadn't.

"It just hit me that I'm thinking about children and stuff like kindergarten and school. It's incredibly domestic." The disbelief rang in his voice. "I never would have thought that I would ever be having this kind of conversation." Gerome drew closer. "And I wouldn't if it hadn't been for you."

“Is that a bad thing?” Tucker asked seriously. He wasn’t sure if Gerome was happy about it or not. Tucker swallowed hard and prepared himself for going it alone once again.

“Honestly, I don’t know.” The softness that spread through Gerome’s features told Tucker more than his words. “I mean… you’ll understand soon enough.” He suddenly seemed defeated. “I’m thinking it isn’t… or maybe I hope it isn’t.” He shifted his weight on his feet and ran his hands through his hair. He was nervous. That surprised Tucker. He hadn’t pictured Gerome as a guy who got anxious about anything. “I never imagined myself as someone who would have a family. My own life in that regard was so unconventional and my experiences largely sucked… so I figured I’d always be on my own in that way.”

Tucker could understand that. “Is that what you want?”

“Life doesn’t always deliver what we want,” Gerome answered. “In fact, for me, it often gave me the exact opposite, and I had to make do with what I could get.”

Tucker placed his hand on Gerome’s cheek, gazing into his eyes. Gerome’s nervous movements stopped. “Maybe life is making up for it now. We both had shitty stuff happen to us. So maybe this… what we might have between us… is its way of evening things out. Maybe this is our chance.”

Gerome swallowed and closed his eyes, slightly leaning into Tucker’s hand. “I really hope you’re right.” He stayed like that for a while, and then Gerome’s eyes slid open, and after a quick kiss, he left the apartment.

Tucker stared after him, wondering once again about Gerome’s past and what could make the usually confident man so tentative.

Chapter 11

"SHIT," GEROME swore under his breath as he pulled into the Driftwood on the way to work. He and Tucker had dropped Joshie at Daniel and Richard's condo for the day before going up to the hospital to try to see Cheryl, but they were only told that there was no change in her condition and they couldn't see her because they weren't family. The plan was to drop Tucker at the restaurant. Gerome was not at all happy to pass Bobby Ramone as he pulled in. "Go inside and tell Richard that this guy is hanging around." He tried not to snap, but it was difficult.

"What are you going to do?"

"Have a little talk with our friend here," Gerome answered. He got out and waited until Tucker was inside before striding across the parking lot. “What are you doing here?”

Bobby pulled himself to his full height. “Just coming after what’s mine.”

“And what would that be?” Gerome inquired, raising his eyebrows as he folded his arms over his chest. “As far as I know, there’s nothing that belongs to you here. I suggest you leave and stay away. Go on home.” Gerome made no indication that he knew that Bobby’s residence was at the bottom of the marina. That was just an added bonus.

“Your friend there has something of mine, and I’m going to get it if I have to take it out of his hide. You better tell him that I’m not going to stop. I’ll follow him until he gives it to me.” Menace dripped from his voice, but Gerome knew guys like this. It didn’t faze him in the least.

“Are you so sure he has whatever it is you seem to have lost?” Gerome half smiled. “You don’t have a fucking clue, do you? What did you lose? Something valuable that doesn’t really belong to you?” He was skirting as close to the edge as he dared, but the spark of fear told him all he needed to know. This guy was grasping at straws, and he was scared half to death. He probably had every right to be if the Garvics were in any way associated with this.

“He has to—” Bobby began.

“No one can give you what they don’t have.” Gerome narrowed his gaze. “But what I can give you is more hurt than you can possibly imagine. I suggest you get the hell out of here and leave him alone. Leave us all alone.”

Bobby scoffed and curled his lip, displaying bleached teeth. “You don’t know what hurt is until I come after you. And I will." He took a step back. "Tell your friend to give me what I want, and nothing will happen to him or the kid." The smile was pure evil, and it sent a chill down Gerome's spine that he did his best not to let show.

"If you hurt either of them," Gerome growled, "I'll hunt you the fuck down and use you for target practice, and I'm a damned good shot." He turned away and strode back to the restaurant. He purposely didn't turn around, even as he braced for some sort of attack. It didn't come, and he went right inside, where Richard met him.

"I see our friend is still here." Richard turned away from the window.

"He's scared shitless, probably because he's on the hook for money he doesn't have. This guy is backed into a corner, and we need to make sure he stays there."

"I was thinking we need to try to find him an out, preferably one that gets him out of the area," Richard whispered. "He's lost his money and his home, probably the drugs he was running. Bobby Ramone isn't going to be popular with his superiors right about now. So maybe a little more attention on the guy will get him fitted for a pair of cement shoes and a plot at the bottom of a swamp."

"How?"

"I'll ask Terrance to see if we can find where this guy is living now. Make him persona non grata there as well." He grinned. "His friends have to be at the point where they'll be ready to cut him loose. We just have to sever the last tie." Richard turned away from the front window. "Go on ahead to work. We'll talk later." He patted Gerome's shoulder. "By the way, how is Joshie doing?"

"Pretty sad. We tried to see Cheryl, but all we got was a condition report like they'd give the media or something. At least she's still alive, so that's good." Gerome hated how the worry was ripping Tucker up. Everything seemed so difficult right now. "Tucker needs someone gentle and caring right now."

"I made sure the kitchen staff knows what he's going through, though he's been a trooper." Richard headed toward the kitchen, and Gerome left to go to work, watching the area around him for anyone who might be lurking.

BASICALLY, GEROME hated January. The store was immaculate, and still he had nothing to do. Gerome hated being bored, and he sat behind the counter, watching the front door, willing someone—anyone—to come into the store. The door stayed closed, and he watched out the front window.

Unusual movement between cars caught his eye. Someone was trying to sneak around the parking lot. Gerome messaged Terrance and got an immediate response that he was on his way. He kept messaging him, explaining the movement and where their watcher was located.

Bobby Ramone suddenly stood up with something in his hand just across from the store and immediately went down again. Gerome wasn't sure if he'd thrown anything, but he hunkered down behind the counter. He expected glass breaking and God knew what else, but nothing happened.

Gerome stood and looked around, and then looked out the window to see Bobby Ramone lying on the ground with a rock in one hand and a lit flare burning on the concrete nearby. The bastard.

Gerome called the police, and they showed up relatively quickly, taking custody of Bobby from Terrance and escorting him away. It seemed that he was out of commission, and his friends definitely weren't going to be coming to his rescue.

"They were happy to get their hands on him," Terrance said once the police left and he'd hurried into the store. "It seems they had been trying to find him since his boat burned, and with the residue they found, they were more than a little interested." He at least seemed pleased. "Come on, I got here in time, and the police have him with the goods ready to try to burn out the store. He isn't going anywhere for quite a while, and if the friends they already have start talking, the whole thing is going to come down around their ears. Everyone left in the group is going to scatter as far away from here as they can get, and we're going to be just fine."

"Except the police have your name in the file, and that's going to reach Elizabeth," Gerome explained. "And we're going to be right in the center of this mess." Not that there was anything they could do about it now. He wasn't angry at Terrance but at himself. He should have done what they always said they were going to do: keep their heads down and out of sight.

"No one recognized us, and in a few days the threat should be gone." Terrance shrugged, and Gerome hoped he was right. But Gerome still thought this was too damned easy and that he and all the guys needed to be careful. If anyone from Garvic's organization was in the area, then they were too close for comfort. And if Elizabeth got word of it, they would indeed be out of town… fast.

"I need to call my boss and let her know what happened," Gerome said. "Thanks for having my back."

"Always," Terrance said, and they bumped fists. Then Terrance strode out of the store on his way to work, and Gerome made his call to his boss.

"YOU NEED to come to the house as soon as you get out of work. The shit is going to hit the fan," Richard said as soon as Gerome answered his call. "Elizabeth is about ready to kill all of us."

"Shit," Gerome murmured just as the front door of the store opened and a group of customers came in. As they wandered the store, Gerome told Richard he'd be there. Then he went to help the ladies. This was not good. Gerome tried to figure out how they were going to put lipstick on this pig.

He finished the rest of his workday and picked up Tucker, and they went right to Richard's. He hadn't had a chance to explain things to Tucker yet, and it looked like his past was going to come crashing down on both of them.

"How bad is this going to be?" Tucker asked. "Richard has been growly and angry-looking all day."

Gerome sighed. "I don't know," he answered honestly.

"Does this have something to do with what you have promised to talk to me about?" Tucker pressed, folding his arms over his chest. "Are your secrets about to come home to roost?" The chill in his voice was unmistakable.

"I'm afraid so… in a way…." He groaned. "This was not how I wanted to talk to you about this, and I would have liked to have spared you and Joshie all of it. Bobby Ramone tried to firebomb the store today, and Terrance caught him. The police have him in custody."

"That's good, right?" Tucker asked.

"Well, yes, it is. But he was involved with some other men, and that boat that we saw pass under the bridge, you know they were running drugs." He tried to explain each piece of the puzzle so he had it all. "We checked out the boat and, well, it just happened to go up in flames and sink to the bottom of the marina, as has Ramone's boat, leaving plenty of evidence." Gerome pulled into the parking lot but left the engine running. This was not the ideal place to tell Tucker all of this, but he didn't have much choice. He wasn't going to let him go into this blind. "What we hoped was that losing their assets would send these guys scurrying away."

"Did it?"

"That's part of what I think we're going to find out. See, these guys have links to the Garvic organization in Detroit."

Tucker glared at him. "And how do you know all this?"

"Because the three of us, Richard, Terrance, and I, used to be members of that organization. We turned state's evidence, and the government put us here. Well, Iowa first, but then here. Terrance saw one of Garvic's operatives a week ago, but there hasn't been anyone since that knows who we are, and it seems the one who did is now gone."

Tucker was silent. The only sound in the car, other than the fan and engine, was Tucker's breathing. "And you got me and Joshie involved in all this?" His nostrils flared and his eyes grew as hard as granite. "How could you?"

"I was trying to protect you. Bobby Ramone would have hurt you, Cheryl, or Joshie without too much thought. I got you away from him more than once. I didn't mean to pull you into our world. I just wanted to help you out, and then I wanted to try to protect you. That's why I didn't tell you anything. As long as you didn't know, you could walk away and never be the wiser. But then Ramone kept coming after you, and you sort of got under my skin, and I didn't want you to go."

Tucker relaxed a little. "What did you do for the Garvics? Did you kill people?"

Gerome didn't answer the question directly. "We ran the gay vices in Detroit. Clubs and rent boys, things like that. All three of us worked together. Richard managed clubs, I helped develop new enticements, and Terrance was the muscle. When we heard they were going to turn on us, we turned them in, and now they are looking for us. So far we haven't been found, and we don't intend to be. Their assets in this area have been destroyed, and the police are onto them."

"But you don't know what's going to happen. And if there are people in the area who know you, then they're going to move you. What happens then?" Tucker demanded. "You made a life possible for me, Cheryl, and Joshie, and now you'll be gone and we'll be all alone again. How fucking fair is that? You get our hopes up that you'll be there, and you get us to really care for you, and then what? We wake up one day and you're just gone and that's the end of it. Do we even have a choice in anything, or did you take those all away from us?"

"Whoa," Gerome said as gently as he could. "I did what I did to try to protect you. I'm sorry about the rest." He understood Tucker's anger, and he probably deserved it. He was completely flying blind and trying to figure things out as he went. "I did something truly good for the first fucking time in my life because I care for you. I didn't want you to know about all of this so you wouldn't get dragged in."

Tucker took a deep breath. "You care for me?"

"Yeah, I do. I got involved in the first place to try to protect you." He turned in the seat. "Look, I don't get involved in other people's shit. I haven't for years, but I did because I like you." He figured he might as well go for broke. Tucker couldn't be any angrier with him than he was right now. "I survived for years in an environment that was the definition of dog-eat-dog. The only people I relied on were Richard and Terrance. I never let anyone else in… until you."

Tucker's mouth worked, but he didn't say anything. "So this wasn't you feeling sorry for me?"

"No." He reached for Tucker's hand. "I helped because I saw something strong in you. I didn't lie. I do know what it feels like to be alone."

Tucker didn't move his hand, but he didn't pull away either. "At least this explains why you know all this stuff. And Daniel?"

"He and Richard met here and fell in love." Gerome shrugged.

Tucker shook his head. "What are you guys? Like Robin Hood or something? You called yourself that when we first met."

"I don't think we're that altruistic." Gerome wasn't really sure what to call himself. This entire situation had opened his eyes and changed him, and now some of the basic truths about himself had shifted. "We're former mobsters in witness protection, and I think we've come to like it here."

Tucker nodded slowly. "Do you miss your old life?"

"Hell yes. It was the life I knew, and it was exciting. We made a lot of money and lived really well. The three of us were respected and feared, so no one messed with us. We ran our business and provided cover for parts of the rest of the organization, though that part of things was Richard's genius. He was great at making the books sing. Me, I was good at business ideas and helping bring them to fruition." He sighed. "It was a great time in my life, but I know that's over and it isn't coming back again." He stared forward at the front of the dark brown building with uninspiring tan trim.

"I get that, but would you go back if you could? Right now, if given the choice, would you?" Tucker asked.

For the first time since entering witness protection, when it came to that question, Gerome hesitated. For months after leaving, he had hoped and even looked for a way to return to his old life.

"I see." Tucker lowered his gaze. "Look, I'll get us packed, and Joshie and I will find a place and get out of your life. I'll look after him until something happens with Cheryl."

"No." Gerome snapped his head around to where Tucker squirmed in his seat. "I'm shitty with explaining these kinds of things, but I can't go back to that life. I wouldn't fit in there anymore, and there would be too many people that I would have to leave behind." He touched Tucker's chin. "People I wouldn't be able to just walk away from. I used to want to go back because living in Detroit and being part of the 'family' made me feel like I was part of something. I haven't felt that way, except with the guys, ever in my whole life… until now." He swallowed and turned away. This was getting to be a little too much. "We should go inside and find out what's going on."

Tucker shook his head. "Is that your way of covering up because you feel something for us?"

"Of course I feel something for you, and I would choose you over my old life every time. But I'm afraid that parts of my old life are going to make an appearance, and the lot of us are going to have to figure all this shit out before it blows up in our faces." He turned off the engine and leaned across the console. Gerome didn't initiate the kiss but waited for Tucker to do it. Then they went inside to face the music.

"GO AHEAD and sit down," Richard said without much greeting once he opened the door. Joshie hurried over to hug Richard, Terrance, and Daniel.

"I'm going to sit with the boys while you talk," Daniel said, flashing Richard a look, like he had better fix this and fast. Then he took Coby and Joshie by the hand. "We can go watch Mickey Mouse."

Joshie hesitated, so Tucker went along with him, lifting Joshie into his arms and carrying him along.

"Did you talk to Tucker?" Richard asked, and Gerome nodded. "I figured, considering how long you were in the car."

"Nothing like leaving things to the last minute." Terrance added his own two cents.

"He's been having a hard time with Cheryl in the hospital and caring for Joshie. I didn't want to add more troubles." He sighed. It didn't matter what his intentions were—trouble had come to pay a visit regardless. "What's the deal?"

"Elizabeth was nearly livid about what's been happening. We of course didn't tell her about the actions we've taken, but she's pissed that we didn't tell her about the drug encroachment. I did tell her that we didn't want to move and have done our best to remain out of sight." That was most definitely a stretch. "She's contacting other agencies and is having them look into the situation. When I spoke with her an hour ago, she seemed to agree that the operation in the area was essentially dead. She was concerned about people who might recognize us."

"Of course she was," Terrance offered. "Like we all aren't."

"What about Tucker and Joshie? What are we supposed to do about them? If we go, they'll be hanging in the wind." That was something he couldn't allow to happen.

Richard nodded. "We're staying where we are. The marshals are going to continue to monitor the situation… for now. But Elizabeth is getting a little nervous."

"What do we do?" Terrance asked.

Richard met each of their gazes in turn. "Nothing at all. We stay out of sight and draw no attention to ourselves. We already took enough actions to expose all of us, and that could have led local law enforcement right to us. Instead, they took the bait and have brought the scrutiny of the law on the threats to us."

"We got exactly what we wanted to happen," Gerome clarified. He really didn't think this was that bad a situation.

"Yes and no. It's possible that someone will figure out that there is someone here on the key who didn't want these guys here, and if that happens, then they could come looking for us. We need to be quiet and stay out of sight at all costs." His voice was hard as rock. "No unilateral operations, and don't get involved with anything. We also need to be vigilant. You know that law enforcement never gets everyone. Someone is still out there, and they'll be watching just as much as we are." Richard stalked closer to Gerome. "You know just as well as I do that Garvic Junior, or whoever is acting in his place, isn't going to just walk away. They don't run scared. They'll try to figure shit out and then get even. That's how things work. Remember?" His tone was as sharp as broken glass.

Gerome did remember. It was the way the three of them had done things whenever someone tried to step into their territory. "Then we have to protect ourselves."

"The easiest fucking way to do that is for us to all relocate. But Daniel doesn't want that, and it isn't good for Coby. I also don't think you want to just uproot and go either. So we fucking stay low, work, and do not under any circumstances draw attention to ourselves. If we see anyone or anything that might be out of the ordinary, we call Elizabeth and let her handle it. Don't do shit on your own, like setting boats on fire and any other shit." His eyes blazed. "What you did could put all of us in jeopardy, and believe me, relocating you would be a piece of cake. If Garvic gets an inkling that we're here, they will kill all of us—Daniel, Tucker, even Coby and Joshie—just to send a fucking message." Richard heaved for breath. "Is that clear?"

Gerome swallowed and nodded, even though he had the instinct to fight Richard on principle. He knew he was fucking right, and if anyone else had spoken to him that way, he would have ripped their throat out, but dammit, he was fucking right. Gerome hated that so damned much. "Fine."

"Terrance?" Richard demanded.

"Fuck," he ground out between his teeth. "Yeah."

Richard took a deep breath. "And now that we have that little bit of business out of the way…." He left the room and returned with Daniel, Tucker, and the boys.

"Have you had your little 'come to Jesus' meeting?" Daniel asked.

"Where's Jesus?" Coby asked, looking around. It was cute, and Gerome smiled, grateful for anything to break the tension.

"Yes. Everything is okay." Richard put his arm around Daniel, drawing him closer. "It's going to be okay. We just need to be smart and not mess things up."

Daniel smiled and turned to Richard. "You need to take your own advice as well." He bumped Richard's hip.

Tucker lifted Joshie onto his lap. "Would you like to start going to school now? They have preschools and things, and you might really like it. There are other kids who will be there, and you get to color and learn your ABCs and 123s." He smiled and hugged Joshie when he agreed. "You're becoming such a big boy."

"Will Mommy go too?" Joshie asked.

Tucker took a deep breath. "Your mommy is in the hospital, and she's too big for school. This is something that is special for kids. When your mommy is feeling better, we'll talk to her about getting you started. Okay?" He smiled and Gerome nodded. They needed to be positive and maintain a good attitude for Joshie's sake. If the worst happened, they would have to deal with it.

"But what if Mommy never gets better?" Joshie whispered, and a lump formed in Gerome's throat.

"Then Tucker will take you to school, and he'll be there to pick you up, and I'll come with you too if you want. But your mom is going to get better, and she loves you very much." Gerome met Tucker's gaze, still unsure how he really felt. Tucker had seemed to accept everything he had explained in the car, but it had been a lot. And yes, Tucker had kissed him, so that was good, but.... He kept coming back to the fact that his life and the implications of it were more than anyone could digest in a few minutes. What Tucker really thought could be something very different.

Joshie buried his face against Tucker's chest, and he held him.

"Everything will work out," Daniel said gently. "She's hanging in there, and we need to give her time and not give up."

Yes." He smiled and tried to believe that a happy outcome was possible, but his gut told him something else entirely. The longer things went on this way, the worse the outlook.

Tucker nodded, gently rubbing Joshie's back, and Gerome slid closer to him, wanting to try to comfort Tucker. He wasn't sure if he'd be allowed, but when Tucker leaned on him slightly, Gerome silently heaved a breath of relief.

"Do you want to play?" Coby asked, and Joshie nodded, wiping his eyes and getting down to play with Coby on the tile floor.

"I'm so grateful," Tucker said quietly. "He needs someone to play with." He watched Joshie, and Gerome wished he could take away this worry for both of them. He could do a lot of things, but that wasn't one of them, any more than he could have changed the outcome when his own mother was terminally ill.

"We're all here for one another," Daniel said. "I know that Gerome has told you things, and I'm glad. But knowing means that you're one of us. We are all party to that secret, and we all survive together by looking after each other."

"Thanks, but I'm not one of you. How do you… live with all of this?" Tucker seemed nervous as hell.

Gerome wished he could provide all the answers Tucker needed, but that wasn't possible, and all he could do was be there. Tucker, on the other hand, had a choice.

"Normally I don't think about it too much because it doesn't come up all the time. I mean, Richard and I lead a pretty normal life, if you discount Frick and Frack over there who are always hanging out and drinking the beer." Gerome considered flipping Daniel off, but then again, he took the bottle of beer that Terrance offered, so that kind of muted his protest. "Only you can decide what you want. But understand this. If you decide that you want to walk away, there isn't going to be a second chance. These three are loyal, and they look after the people in their lives. However, if you decide to leave and then realize what you could have had later, it will be too late. All of us will be gone, moved to a different portion of the country, and you'll never find any of us."

"You'd all move because of me?" Tucker asked.

Daniel shared a look with Richard. "We won't have any choice. The government will find places for all of us, and one day we'll be gone and living in separate places." He shrugged. "I don't say this to scare you or warn you off. I don't want to influence you, but that's one of the facts of life around here. We all know it, and that's what keeps everyone in line." Daniel turned to Gerome with a gentle expression that Gerome didn't really understand. "Or at least it did until this guy decided that he was going to go out on a limb for you."

Tucker swallowed hard and met Gerome's gaze. "It's hard for me to reconcile the man you were with the one I know." He blinked, and Gerome moved to stand next to him.

"The guy I was before, in Detroit, is still me, I guess. It's hard for me to explain. I'm the same and yet I'm not. I have a regular job and I've never, ever skimmed a cent from it. The people who hired us took chances, and we protect the people in our lives." He took Tucker's hand. "We've never hurt innocent people, not once. And we certainly didn't go around shooting up the town or killing people in revolving doorways like they show in the movies. But we eliminated our rivals and protected the folks who worked for us." He tried to explain things as clearly as he could.

"All this is so much to take in." Tucker seemed pale but held his head high.

Gerome could almost feel Tucker pulling away, and he didn't know what to do about it. He had resisted telling him about himself in part because he was afraid of just this reaction. Not that he could blame Tucker. It was a lot to take in to find out that the guy in your life was in hiding and had a pretty intense history.

"Of course it is. It was for me too. What I did was look at the man I knew." Daniel's gaze shifted to Richard and his expression completely changed. His face grew softer and his eyes more intense, filling with deep love that Gerome hoped he would see one day. "Richard stood up for me and put himself and his safety between me and the world. He didn't fill my ears with words, but he did show me that he truly loved me and Coby. The thing is that any decision about what you want to do is yours alone." Finally, Daniel returned his attention to Tucker. "You have to make the best decision for you and Joshie. But I will tell you this. You will look a long time before you find anyone else who is willing to put their own safety in jeopardy in order to help you or anyone else." Daniel looked around. "I'm going to check on the boys." He left the room, and Gerome figured they had all had enough of this for the night.

"Do you want to go home?" he asked Tucker, who nodded. He figured there was only so much any of them could say at this point, and Tucker needed a chance to make up his own mind.

There were few things that Gerome hated more than having his life out of his control. Over the past few years, he had gotten more used to the fact that there were many things that he couldn't influence. As much as he wanted to plead his case to Tucker, this was one of the times when he needed to accept whatever happened, even if it might leave him completely hollowed out. Gerome had fallen in love with Tucker—he had no doubt of that. He looked forward to every single second they spent together, and he hated when they went their separate ways.

Joshie ran down the hall and barreled into Tucker. "Coby asked me if I can sleep over."

Tucker bit his lower lip and seemed worried. In that moment, Gerome understood just how much this entire situation had rocked Tucker on his heels. A war seemed to be brewing behind Tucker's eyes, and Gerome knew he was so unsure of what to do. "Sure, if

Mr. Daniel says it's all right," he finally said, probably because of the pleading in Joshie's eyes.

"Of course. I'll bring him home once you're done with work tomorrow." Both Coby and Joshie put their hands in the air like they had won some contest and then hurried off to play once more. "And don't worry. I'll call if there are any issues."

Tucker nodded. "I keep worrying that things will remind him of his mother and…."

Gerome put an arm around his shoulder. "I wish I could take all that away."

Tucker lifted his gaze. "I know you do. But that's one thing that none of us can do." He leaned his head against Gerome's side.

Daniel smiled up at him. "I'm going to get a few snacks together." He went into the kitchen and returned with chips and crackers. "You guys need to eat if you're going to drink, because I'm not hauling any of you to bed."

"I need to go into the store early tomorrow for inventory, so I can't have another beer after this one," Terrance said as he took a handful of chips.

"I'll alert the media that the beer supply is safe for another day," Daniel teased, and Terrance fake growled at him, stuffing his mouth full of chips, and then washed it down with the last of his beer. At least some things were normal.

Gerome followed Tucker as he wandered into the small bedroom where the boys were playing to say goodbye to Joshie. He sat on the floor intently running a truck through a makeshift obstacle course. "I'll see you after work tomorrow," Tucker said softly, and Joshie jumped to his feet and hurried over. Tucker hugged him and seemed to try not to get teary-eyed. "Will you promise to be good?"

Joshie nodded against his shoulder. "I be good." He held him for a long time. Tucker didn't seem to want to let him go, but eventually Joshie went back to playing, and Tucker watched until Gerome lightly tapped him on the shoulder.

Chapter 12

TUCKER GOT out of the car and waited for Gerome. He wasn't sure what he should do or even what he wanted. The past few hours had passed in a kind of blur where he vacillated between wanting to be comforted by Gerome and wanting to pull away and try to figure things out on his own. Gerome was a mobster… former mobster… whatever. That whole thing had left him unsettled. He kept wondering if that person was still inside and if Gerome would go back to that kind of life. Did he want to? Tucker couldn't take that. Though that did explain an awful lot about how Gerome and the guys knew the stuff they did.

Hell, he was so fucking confused that Joshie was having a sleepover at Daniel and Richard's. He kept wondering if he should go back and say that he made a mistake and bring Joshie home. Yet Gerome and the guys had been nothing but nice to him, and they had protected him and made sure he would be able to keep Joshie. How could he be angry about that?

"Hey, I can almost feel the whiplash of your thoughts," Gerome said as he guided Tucker inside his apartment.

"How could you do this to me?" Tucker asked. "I finally meet a guy who cares about me and stands up for me—something my parents didn't fucking do—and I find out that he's a criminal… was a criminal… I don't fucking know what the hell you are. How do I get my head around all this?" He glared at Gerome.

"I don't know. I can't give you that answer." Gerome sat down, leaning forward, his gaze on his shoes, as though they might start talking and provide the answer. "All I can tell you is that I'm the guy I've always been. Yeah, I have one hell of a past, but that's my past. I'm the same guy who you went with to scope out that boat and the one who you dragged along to wait on the bridge. I'm the guy who raced to that camp to make sure you were safe when I realized you were being followed." He grew quiet, and Tucker had to give him credit, because Gerome was the reason he and Joshie had a place to live. And just like he'd promised, Gerome had never asked for anything in return. That was part of the reason Tucker had fallen for the guy. He was truly kind.

"I feel kind of betrayed," Tucker said softly. "I don't know how else to feel. It's like you were being nice to us and now I found out this… past… isn't what I thought." He sighed and sat down as well. "I know that no one should be judged for his past, and I don't want you judging me for mine, but this is hard for me to get my head around." He wished he could just gloss over all of this, but he couldn't. It was something he needed to process and try to reconcile somehow.

Gerome nodded. "I think I understand. But try to see things from my perspective. I couldn't tell you earlier because this isn't just my secret. It's Richard's and Terrance's too. It also affects Daniel and Coby. I have to think of them and be careful. If you decide you want to tell someone or can't keep our secret, then we all get split up and moved somewhere else. I know Daniel explained that to you."

Tucker nodded and took Gerome's hand. "No matter what, I will be quiet and tell no one. I don't want to hurt any of you. I just need a chance to think about all this." He leaned down and kissed Gerome on the forehead. "I need to go home and get to bed."

Gerome met his gaze, looking puzzled, or maybe hurt.

"I don't hate you, and I'm not angry with you. I understand why you did what you did. But I have to be able to figure some things out, and I can't do that with you here. You distract me way too much, and this is something I need a clear head for." Tucker squeezed Gerome's hand and then went across the hall to his apartment. He closed and locked the door, instantly alone.

The temptation to go back across the hall was strong. Very strong. He knew he had set his heart on Gerome, but it wasn't just what he wanted that counted anymore. He had to think about what was best for Joshie, too, and Joshie deserved a stable life with friends and school and all the things a kid needed. Tucker was going to have to figure out college, and Joshie deserved a room of his own, and.... The past few days settled on his shoulders like a block of concrete.

Maybe being alone wasn't such a great idea. The apartment was empty and quiet—*super* quiet. He turned on the television just for some noise to drown out the racing thoughts. What the hell was he going to do?

No grand answer flooded into his head like some magic insight. He kept going back to what he thought was right, but even that was muddled. Tucker knew it wasn't fair to hold Gerome's past against him, but he also wondered how much of his mobster past had become part of the person he was.

Maybe he had seen way too many movies and was letting that cloud his judgment. Tucker had no fucking idea what he was going to do. The simple fact was that he should probably run screaming into the night, take Joshie, and figure out a way to live on his own and try to make them both happy. On the other hand, Joshie could possibly be in foster care with strangers if it weren't for Gerome and his friends. They'd looked after Tucker and Joshie, to their own detriment and risk. They hadn't asked for anything in return except maybe Tucker's understanding.

That was all logical, and his head went in circles, but another fact was just as clear: somehow, in some way, he had fallen in love with Gerome. Former gangster or not, Tucker had come to really care for him, and he thought Gerome felt the same way. He had no doubt that Gerome would never hurt either him or Tucker. Hell, he was pretty sure that Gerome would walk through fire for both of them. Maybe that was what he should concentrate on instead of Gerome's past.

Still, he had a hard time letting go of the idea of what Gerome might have done. Maybe that was the crux of the issue—his damned imagination. Gerome had sidestepped telling him the kinds of things he had done in his past, and now Tucker's mind was filling in the blanks.

He sat back on the sofa and noticed the program he'd started watching had changed. Tucker hadn't even realized how long he had sat there lost in his thoughts. He got up and turned the TV off, made up his bed on the sofa, and slipped under the covers. Hopefully if he slept on it, he could figure out what in the hell he should do.

Tucker lay under the covers, staring up at the ceiling, trying to go to sleep. Like everyone else, whenever he *tried* to sleep, he only lay awake, his head refusing to settle down. He checked the clock after an hour and got up again.

Tucker pulled on a pair of shorts and padded to the door, then peered outside into the hall. Lying awake, he had pretty much come to the conclusion that he wasn't going to get any answers from his own ruminations. The only place he was going to get what he needed was from Gerome.

This was stupid. It was nearing midnight. What did he expect, that Gerome would be up and waiting for him? Tucker shook his head and was about to close his door when Gerome's cracked open. "Is something wrong?" Gerome poked his head out and looked both ways. "I heard movement and wanted to make sure no one was sneaking around."

"You couldn't sleep either?" Tucker asked.

Gerome opened his door farther. Tucker grabbed his keys, locked his door, and stepped across the hall. After following Gerome inside, he stood in the living room, unsure what he should do. A million questions raced through his head, but it was late and probably wasn't the best time for Q and A.

"I've been awake for a while. Sleep doesn't seem to happen as easily as when you're here with me."

Tucker sighed. "You say things like that and it makes it harder for me to talk about the stuff I need to." He didn't tense as Gerome closed the distance between them. In fact, his heart sped up and his blood raced, sending heat through him. In moments his attention was on the man in front of him, his strength and the way he felt under Tucker's hands. Tucker closed his eyes for a second and suddenly he was lost in Gerome's presence, the way he held him as though the outside world didn't exist. And Gerome hadn't actually done anything or moved another muscle.

"What do you want?" Gerome breathed.

"Answers. I want to know who you are. I want to be able to trust my own instincts." Maybe that was the root of it all. Tucker needed to understand what was real.

Gerome drew nearer, this time clutching Tucker to him. "You already know the real me. More than most anyone else on earth. I haven't hidden who I am from you. No, I didn't tell you about parts of my past, but I showed you the man that I am. I let you see the real me. Not the things I've done but the person I am inside and what I feel." Gerome swallowed, and damn, Tucker wanted that to be the truth, so much he could taste it. Then he could… as Gerome kissed him.

"I…," Tucker muttered seconds later as Gerome pulled away.

"Yes?" Gerome backed away and motioned to the sofa. "What do you want to know?"

Tucker could feel the moment between them withering, but he wasn't going to be dissuaded by Gerome's sexiness. He sat down with Gerome next to him.

"Before the three of us arrived here, we did what we had to do in Detroit. We protected each other, the business, and our territory as well as the people we worked for. That was our job. Sometimes we did things that maybe we wished we hadn't. When the old boss passed away and his son took over, we realized that he wasn't interested in having any sort of gay business. Instead of just divesting it, he decided to take us down, but we got to him first."

"You turned state's evidence?" Tucker asked.

"Yes." Gerome slid closer. "See, our lives were built on loyalty. We look after each other, and the people we work for are supposed to take care of us. We were betrayed, so we took them down. After testifying, we were moved to Iowa, and then here." He sighed. "All three of us grew up on the streets, and we've watched after each other since we were about ten years old. Tough kids who grew into tough adults." He sighed as Tucker tried to reconcile all this with the person he knew. The thing was, it jelled pretty well. Gerome was loyal, and he was fiercely protective. That was crystal clear.

"But you did bad things," Tucker prompted. He had to know.

"Yes. We did some bad things." The expression in his eyes was a strange cocktail of pride and caution. "We did them to protect what was ours. Pure and simple. And I will do what I need to in order to protect what I have now. So, let me try to explain. In Detroit, we ran clubs and other operations. We kept books that were works of art, and fake as hell. We helped hide income from other operations and put people on the payroll to help cover up other income. Richard was a master at it. There was a steady flow of dirty money that came through the clubs and came out relatively clean. All three of us have jobs here now. We have never taken a cent that doesn't belong to us. We protect the people we work for, and we don't steal from them." The pride in Gerome's voice rang through as he leaned closer. "We also forged a statement from Cheryl so Joshie could stay with the person he cares for, and given the choice, we would do it over again… for you… for Joshie… and a little for myself, because I want the people I love to be happy."

Tucker stared. Had Gerome just said what he thought he heard? "You love me?" he whispered.

"Yes. I love you, and I hope that maybe if you can see your way clear, that maybe someday I can be Joshie's other dad. I know you have things that you need to work out, and I also know that I danced around some of your questions. But that part of my life is over, and I don't want to taint you with what I did."

"Just answer this. Did you ever kill someone?" Tucker asked. He had to know.

Gerome shook his head. "No. I never killed anyone." He stood up. "Look, it's really late, and we both need to work tomorrow. You can stay here with me if you like, or you can go home. It's up to you." There was hope in Gerome's eyes, but Tucker wasn't sure how much sleep he would get if he stayed.

Tucker felt better about where things stood between them. A lot of his questions, or at least the worst of his fears, had been answered. "Let's go on to bed." He took Gerome's hand, and when the lights were out, let him lead through the apartment to the bedroom. They were both tired, and once under the covers, Gerome held him tightly, his scent surrounding him. Tucker closed his eyes, his mind settled and quiet, and soon sleep carried him away.

"YOU NEED to pay attention," Zane said, and Tucker pulled his attention out of his thoughts. "I don't want you to cut off your fingers." The guy actually smiled, and Tucker put his head down to get back to his task. The vegetable prep for salads was the last item on his list for the day, and he was looking forward to going home. Gerome had said he was going to take him and Joshie out for dinner, and Tucker was really looking forward to it.

Once he'd finished, Tucker cleaned his area and made sure all his utensils were washed up and put away. Zane was doing his final dinner prep, and it seemed to him that they were just about ready, which was where Tucker liked things to be when he left.

"I'll see you tomorrow," he told Zane. He grabbed his things and headed out through the back kitchen door. Daniel had arranged to pick him up after work, so he went around to the parking lot.

Pain bloomed on his back, and the ground came up to meet him. He managed to cushion his fall and rolled over. Bobby Ramone loomed over him with a knife. "You make a sound and I'll cut you to pieces." He yanked Tucker to his feet and pressed the blade to his side. "You start walking slowly right through those trees."

Tucker barely breathed as the point nicked his side. He realized he was being led to one of the cars, and once he was inside, he would have no way out, and who knew where he was going to be taken. But he had no choice.

Chapter 13

GEROME SNATCHED his phone off the table.

"He isn't here," Daniel said with a touch of panic in his voice. "I'm at the Driftwood, and Zane said Tucker left fifteen minutes ago. He went out the back and hasn't been seen since. I've got the boys in the car." Now he seemed to be more upbeat, and Gerome knew it was an act.

"I'm on my way," Gerome said. "The store is dead, so I'm going to lock up and come right over." He hung up, put the cash in the safe, and bolted out the door, flipping the Closed sign before hurrying off to his car. It was only a few minutes early anyway. He raced to the restaurant and pulled to a stop, grabbed the tire iron out of the trunk, then hurried around the back. He checked out the area and saw nothing.

Inside, he talked with Zane for a few seconds, but he had been at work the entire time. Continuing through, he found Daniel and the boys at a table. They were having a snack, and Gerome greeted them all before continuing out the front and then walking the area around the building.

Something glinted in the scraggly grass near the next parking lot, and Gerome hurried over. It was Tucker's name badge. At least he knew Tucker had come this way.

Gerome continued across the parking lot, hoping for some other clue. He had to find Tucker. There was no telling what these assholes would do if they had him, and damn it all, the thought of anyone hurting him had Gerome ready to punch one of the fucking palm trees.

"Gerome!"

He shifted his gaze just in time to see Tucker being shoved into a car. Holy hell, he was still here! Gerome might have arrived in time. He raced across the parking lot as Bobby Ramone jumped around his car toward the driver's side. The guy was some kind of idiot, because Tucker jumped out and rolled away, taking shelter behind the next vehicle.

The engine sputtered and didn't turn over right away. Ramone slammed his hands into the steering wheel as Gerome leaned against the other car on the driver's side, bashing in the window with everything he had. The engine caught as Gerome reached inside, half yanking Ramone out of the opening before he could put the Lexus in gear. "You move and I'll rip your fucking head off."

"Gerome!" Tucker called weakly.

"I got him," Richard said, pulling out his phone as he approached Tucker from the Driftwood. "It's okay. Gerome, give me your shirt. Tucker is bleeding."

Gerome yanked his shirt, buttons flying, and tossed the remains to Richard one-handed without letting go of the asshole.

"He stole from me," Ramone protested.

Gerome leaned damned close to him. "You piece of shit. He never did anything to you." He wanted to snap the asshole's neck, but sirens approached, so he held him tight, occasionally looking at Tucker, who was growing paler on the ground, Gerome's once-white shirt slowly turning red where it was pressed to his side. "And if anything happens to him, I will find you and make sure you never, ever walk right again."

The police arrived, and Gerome explained what had happened, turning Bobby Ramone over to them. As soon as it was safe, he rushed to Tucker, whose breathing was a little ragged. Gerome hoped to hell that whatever he had been stabbed with hadn't reached his lung. "It's going to be okay. I'm here." He held Tucker's hand as Richard kept the cloth in place.

An ambulance arrived, and Gerome stayed with Tucker as the EMTs started working on him. "Gerome...," Tucker whispered. "Take care of Joshie...," he gasped.

Gerome clutched his hand. "Don't worry. I'll be here."

"Please relax and lie still," the EMT said as they called in to the hospital, relaying the information they gathered. Gerome filled in as much as he knew, and they readied Tucker for transport.

Gerome could hardly breathe. He had seen guys beaten up and injured since he was a kid, but none of them meant as much as the man they were about to lift into the ambulance. He hadn't felt this lost since the last day he'd seen his mother.

"I'll take you to the hospital," Richard offered.

"I need to get Joshie and see that he's all right." He got up, watching as Tucker was closed into the back of the ambulance.

"We're transporting him to St. Michael's," the EMT interrupted.

"We'll be there," Gerome said. He hurried back toward the restaurant as the ambulance pulled out of the parking area, its siren sounding.

Daniel and the boys met him with the car at the front door of the restaurant, and he got in. Gerome wasn't in any shape to drive, and Joshie was already in a car seat in Daniel's back seat. "Where's Tucker?" Joshie asked quietly.

"He got hurt," Gerome said, turning around. "We're going to the hospital so we can see how he is."

Joshie began to whimper. "Is he sick like Mommy?"

Gerome's heart cracked wide open. "I was just with him, and he's going to be okay. He just got hurt, and the doctors are going to make him better." God, he hoped he wasn't going to end up a liar. Gerome didn't know what he'd do if anything happened to Tucker. Sweat broke out all over, and his legs shook as Daniel drove.

"Do you promise?" Joshie asked, still whimpering.

Gerome wished he could get back there with him to try to comfort Joshie. "I do. I promise." Gerome felt his own tears prickling, his throat closing up. "We're going to get there as fast as we can so we can see him and your mommy. Okay? I promise we won't leave until you can hold both their hands." He fully intended to keep that promise if he had to tear the hospital apart with his fists. Joshie wasn't going to be hurt again.

Daniel pulled up in front of the hospital, and Gerome got out. "Thank you."

"Do you want us to stay?" Daniel asked, leaning slightly over the seat.

"I'll get us a cab home." It was going to be a while; Gerome was sure of that. There was no need for Coby and Daniel to sit around the hospital for hours.

"No way. Just call and one of us can pick you up," Daniel told him.

Gerome thanked him and closed the door. He got Joshie out of the back seat, lifting him into his arms. After waving, he carried Joshie inside the emergency entrance.

"We're here for Tucker Wells. He was just brought in by ambulance. This is his nephew, and I'm his boyfriend. He was hurt, and we need to see him." Gerome's sight narrowed, and he held Joshie tightly, hugging him in order to try to calm himself down. "We also need to see Cheryl Henning. She's Joshie's mother."

"Yes," the receptionist said. "Please have a seat a minute." She motioned to the chairs in the damned waiting area, and Gerome sat down. Joshie didn't show any sign of wanting to get down, so Gerome held him on his lap.

"It smells funny," Joshie said.

"I know. Hospitals always smell like disinfectant and stuff. It means it's clean and that Tucker isn't going to get germs." He made a face, and Joshie giggled slightly. It was good to hear that sound, even if it was stressed.

"Sir. He's awake, and you can go back to see him," she said and escorted them through a secure door to a room with glass walls.

"What about Cheryl Henning? This is her son, and he'd like to see her." He was determined to try to let Joshie see his mother.

"I checked, and she isn't able to have visitors at the moment because of the hour, but I'll ask someone to come talk to you." Gerome figured that was the best answer he was going to get.

Tucker lay on a bed, pale but awake. His shirt was gone, probably cut away, and he had a bandage on his side.

"Tucker," Joshie said, hurrying to the bed. Gerome picked him up so he could see better. "Does it hurt bad? Mommy kisses owies and makes them better." He sniffed and turned back to Gerome, holding him as he cried. "I want Mommy." The sound tore at Gerome's heart, and he rubbed Joshie's back.

"Tucker is going to be okay, I promise," Gerome said, rocking gently.

"You're a natural at that," Tucker said with a hiss.

"Have they told you anything?" Gerome asked.

Tucker took a deep breath and winced. "It isn't as bad as they thought. He cut me, but it didn't go too deep. At least they don't think so. I lost some blood and stuff, but none of the organs are affected. It just hurts."

"What's that for?" Joshie asked, pointing to the IV.

"That's so they can make sure I get enough to drink," Tucker said, holding out his arm. Gerome positioned Joshie so he could hug Tucker without putting any weight on him.

A woman came in, explained that she was the doctor, and asked them to step out for a few minutes. Gerome carried Joshie out, and they stood in the hallway.

Gerome found a chair nearby and sat down, Joshie on his lap. He watched the door, waiting. Inside, he was pacing the floor back and forth, but on the outside, he tried to remain calm for Joshie's sake. The sweet little boy had had more than his share of upheaval in the past few weeks, and he didn't need any more.

"Is he going to be okay?" Joshie's blue eyes met his, beseeching him.

"Yes. I think they're working now to help make him better. When they're done, you can go back in to see him." Gerome was just as anxious as Joshie was.

"But I wanna see him now," Joshie protested. "And when can I see Mommy?" He was getting antsy, not that Gerome could blame him.

"I know. Me too." He figured they were going to be a while when a nurse entered the room with a wheeled tray. Fortunately, a curtain had been pulled so they couldn't see what was happening, but Gerome figured that they were stitching Tucker up. God, he hoped so, and that he truly wasn't hurt that badly.

"How long is it going to be?" Joshie asked.

"I don't know." Gerome sighed and kept watching.

Joshie shifted his weight, resting his head on his shoulder. Gerome loved that Joshie trusted him enough to relax. Gerome rubbed his back, and Joshie settled and grew quiet. He didn't know if he was going to go to sleep or not, but at least he seemed to have calmed down. That in itself was a relief.

Half an hour later, they were still waiting. Finally the curtain was shifted back. Gerome got up slowly and carried a dozed-off Joshie into the room with him.

"He's going to be sore for quite some time. We're going to add an antibiotic to his IV, and once that's finished, he should be able to go home. We'll give you some prescriptions for the pain as well as a course of additional antibiotics to help fight off infection." She went through a sheet with a number of aftercare instructions, and Gerome took note of each and every one. He intended to make sure Tucker followed them all to the letter.

The doctor pulled off her gloves and tossed them in the red container. "You were very lucky. The wound was clean and not too deep."

"Thank you, Doctor," Tucker said softly, his eyes drooping closed.

"You're going to need a lot of rest for the next couple of days. Your body is going to be doing a lot of healing, and that is going to take about all the energy you have. For now, just sleep if you want. You're going to be here for a few more hours, and I want to check on the wound one more time before we let you go." She turned to leave.

"Doctor, Joshie here is Cheryl Henning's son. Tucker is his uncle, and we'd like to be able to see her."

She nodded. "Yes. They told me. Visiting hours are over, but Cheryl has improved and she is waking up. I can't go into any details, but I suggest you come tomorrow during visiting hours." She turned to Joshie. "You can see and talk to your mommy then."

Joshie smiled and took Tucker's hand.

Tucker smiled and held it as he closed his eyes once again. Gerome wished he could be the one to hold his hand, but Joshie needed the reassurance. "I'm gonna be okay, Joshie," he whispered. "Maybe you and Gerome can go get a snack. I won't go anywhere. I promise."

"I wanna stay," Joshie said.

Gerome set him down and brought over a chair so Joshie could sit right next to the bed.

"Do you want some juice?" Gerome asked, and when Joshie nodded, he left the room. A nurse showed him where the juice machine was, and he got Joshie a cup with a straw. Joshie hadn't moved a muscle while he was gone, and he took the juice and only let go of Tucker's hand to drink all of it and then hand the Styrofoam cup back to Gerome to throw away.

"Mommy took me to the hospital once," Joshie said.

"She did?" Gerome asked.

Joshie nodded and held up his finger. "I cut it, and they sewed it shut. I was a big boy and didn't really cry."

"You're always a good boy." Tucker squeezed Joshie's hand and closed his eyes. "I'm really tired." He sighed and yawned, closing his eyes. Tucker drifted off to sleep, and Gerome shifted Joshie onto his lap. Joshie watched Tucker, leaning against Gerome's chest.

Gerome wished he knew something to talk about. "You've been so good. Tomorrow, after you see your mommy, maybe you can come to work with me. We have some toys at the store, and you can pick one out." Joshie deserved a treat, and he needed some more things to play with. He was a kid, after all.

"Really?"

"Yeah. We have puzzles and some games." He beat himself up because he probably should have brought some of those toys home for him already. "You can play with them and see what you like." Gerome hugged him and looked over at Tucker. For a few seconds, Gerome felt like they might be making some kind of a family. It was probably a stupid time and a ridiculous place for that kind of realization, but it really felt like it.

It was a shame, and Gerome was sorry that Cheryl had gotten sick. It sucked for Joshie and for all of them. Cheryl was a kind person, and Gerome was coming to understand the value of a little kindness. Hell, he wanted that. His life had been all sharp edges and strength for so long that the thought of kindness and care had been foreign. Now, sitting with Tucker and Joshie, he realized pretty clearly what Richard had seen and felt when he'd met Daniel. To be part of a family. Part of him felt bad to think that he got to experience this because of Cheryl's ill health.

"Is he asleep?" Joshie whispered.

Gerome nodded. "We need to be quiet so he can rest. And when we get home, I think that maybe you and Tucker can come stay with me for a little while. That way, you and I can help him get better."

Joshie sniffed. "And Mommy too." Tears ran down his cheeks.

"Sweetheart, we'll take care of Tucker, your mommy, and everyone else we love. I didn't have someone like Uncle Tucker to take care of me. But you do."

"Or an Uncle Gerome?" Joshie asked. Gerome had to turn away for a second because he was suddenly overwhelmed. The only person who ever called him Uncle Gerome was Coby, and he figured that was where Joshie picked it up, but still… to hear him use it for the first time….

"That's right. The only person I had who was there always was Terrance's mom." He swallowed, suddenly missing her a great deal. "She was nice to me." Joshie watched him as though he were looking for something. "I remember when I was about twelve maybe. Richard, Terrance, and me were on our way home from school." He leaned close as if to share a secret. "I was always really good in school, and so was Richard. Terrance not so much. But we all did our homework together, and we helped him. Anyway, there was a gang of kids who used to beat up the other kids and take their lunch money."

Joshie gasped. "They were mean." He made a face.

Gerome had to agree with him. "Yes, they were. They usually left us alone because we didn't have lunch money, but one day they decided to beat me up, and I came to Terrance's house with a hurt lip and a black eye. His mama was so mad. She went down to that school and gave that principal a talking-to." He smiled. There was nothing like Terrance's mother in full-on protective mother mode. It was a beautiful thing. Gerome thought she might have threatened the principal within an inch of his life. Gerome was never sure, but things were different after that. "Your uncle Tucker is like that. He'll stand up for you always, no matter what. And I will too. I promise you that." He smiled. "Do you know what you want to be when you grow up?" He figured it was a good time to change the subject.

"A fireman," Joshie answered right away. "I wanna drive a fire truck with lights and a siren." He seemed just about to make the sound of a siren, so Gerome put his finger to his lips. Joshie nodded and settled down. Dang, this was an amazing kid.

"That's really good. Firemen do good work." He did notice that it was all about the vehicles. Clearly that was Joshie's thing.

"Tucker?" Joshie asked.

"Hey, buddy," Tucker said softly. "I'm okay." He extended his hand, and Joshie took it. Gerome figured Joshie needed to see that Tucker was okay.

"How much longer?"

"Until the bags over there are empty," Tucker answered. "See, there isn't much left, and once I have all the good juice, then I can probably go home." He shifted and winced. "Though I'm not going to be able to move very much."

"I take care of you," Joshie said.

"Maybe you can be a doctor when you grow up," Tucker offered.

Joshie turned to him. "What kind of car does a doctor get? Does it have a siren?" He bounced on Gerome's lap.

"Nope."

Joshie thought a second. "Then I'm gonna be a fireman."

The nurse entered the area, checked on Tucker's IV, and looked over the bandage. "The bleeding is minimal and the IV is nearly done. I'll check with the doctor, and then we can see about getting your paperwork set before sending you home. You will have someone there to help you, and this big guy, right?"

"Yes. I'll be there." Gerome spoke up and squeezed Tucker's hand lightly. Tucker nodded and closed his eyes once again.

"Is he sleeping?" Joshie asked.

Gerome shook his head. "He's resting, and we need to be quiet. Are you hungry?" He figured if he could get Joshie busy with something, it would occupy him. Joshie grew quiet once again. They waited a while longer until the nurse returned to take out the IV and have Tucker sign his discharge papers. Then they reviewed his home-care instructions again before helping him up off the bed. Since he didn't have a shirt, they gave him a temporary one and got him on his feet.

Tucker moved slowly to the wheelchair, and an orderly wheeled him out of the hospital as Gerome and Joshie waited for Daniel to pick them up. They got Tucker into the front seat, and Gerome wedged himself in the back between the car seats for the drive back to the apartment.

"Are you hungry?" Daniel asked. "I have a cooler in the trunk with some dishes you can warm up in the microwave once you get home."

"Man, you think of everything," Gerome said, gently patting Tucker on the shoulder. He would be much happier once this bumpy drive was over and he got Tucker into bed. Then maybe he could relax a little and Tucker could rest and start to heal. "Do you think you could drop me back at my car? I'll follow you from there." He probably should stop at the store and make sure everything was okay, but he figured he could get everything in the morning.

"No problem," Daniel said as they crossed the bridge onto the key. Gerome climbed out once they reached the Driftwood, and he hurried to his car and followed them back.

"There," Gerome said once he got Tucker inside and into his bed. Joshie climbed up next to him with one of his cars.

"I stay to help you," Joshie pronounced as though he had the last word.

"Let's go get something to eat. You can help me, and then I'll bring in a tray for Tucker," Gerome offered, and Joshie went with him to the kitchen. All Gerome needed to do was heat up some pasta, but he got Joshie to help and let him carry the plate to the bedroom while Gerome brought in the bed tray.

Tucker was waiting, and Gerome and Joshie got him settled with dinner, then joined him on the bed. "You have to eat really carefully," Gerome said. "We don't want to get Tucker dirty."

Joshie ate his macaroni one piece at a time. He was so cute.

"I'm really not that hungry," Tucker said.

"Then eat what you want." Gerome didn't have much of an appetite either, but he stayed close and helped both of them, then took care of the dishes when they were done because it seemed that Joshie didn't intend to go anywhere.

GEROME WOKE in the middle of the night. He carefully got out of the bed. Tucker was asleep, having taken a pain pill that had knocked him out. That was a blessing, because rest was what he needed most. Gerome left the room, quietly making his way to the living room, where Joshie was curled up on the sofa with his well-worn stuffed toy.

"Is everything okay?" Tucker whispered from the other room.

Gerome returned and climbed into bed. "Yeah. I was just checking that Joshie was okay." He settled back under the covers, moving as little as possible in the queen-size bed. He didn't want to disturb, but he also didn't want to be any farther away than necessary. "He's sound asleep."

Tucker hummed and groaned. "I'm not sure what I'm going to do."

"About what?" Gerome settled under the covers, lightly stroking Tucker's arm just because he needed to feel him, to know that he was okay.

"We all need a permanent home," Tucker said.

"That's not a problem. I was thinking of getting a place like Daniel and Richard have. It would be big enough that Joshie and Cheryl could each have their own room, and there would be a decent kitchen and a place for him to play. Maybe one near Daniel and

Richard so there would be people we already know and Joshie could play with Coby."

Tucker shifted and hissed slightly before settling once again. "But where is the money going to come from?"

Gerome thought for a second. "I have plenty of it. Before we left Detroit, I made sure that all three of us were well set up. The money is offshore, but we can bring it back, carefully. It will take some time, but it can be done." He paused. "There's something else that I need to tell you. That package you were supposed to find on the beach… well, I found it."

Tucker didn't move. "You did?"

"Yeah. It's a brick of cash. It's hidden away." Tucker hit him. "Oww. What was that for?"

"Why did you do that?" Tucker whispered.

"Because if we had given it to them, they would have been able to use it to make themselves stronger. As it is, the loss of the money weakened them. And if you had turned that money over to him, you might have gotten what he promised to pay you, but more likely you would have simply disappeared. They weren't going to leave a trail that anyone could follow." Gerome rolled over and threaded Tucker's fingers with his. "I really wanted to spare you all of this."

Tucker closed his eyes and sighed softly. "I don't want to think about that." He shivered, and Gerome moved closer. "I really compounded dumb on top of stupid, didn't I?"

"You were desperate, hungry, and vulnerable. There shouldn't be a crime in that, but he almost pulled you into one." Gerome snuggled closer, desperate to make Tucker feel better and wishing he'd just kept his mouth shut. But he didn't want there to be more secrets between them. There had been plenty already, and he had to clear the air. "But now that we're safe and Bobby Ramone is gone, I was thinking we could use it to help the boys and Cheryl so she can recover. Put this dirty money to good use."

"How?"

Gerome shrugged. "We'll launder the money into their college funds and to pay hospital and any physical therapy bills. That way Cheryl won't have to worry, and both boys have a real chance in life when they get older." He had no idea what to expect, but it wasn't Tucker guiding him closer so he could kiss him. "I thought you'd be mad."

Tucker sighed. "I don't have the energy to be mad, and all I would have done is turn the money over to him anyway. Besides, I like the idea of using that awful money for the boys." He slowly turned toward him. "You know, you really have turned into Robin Hood."

Gerome growled. "Great."

Tucker chuckled softly. "I think I really like that idea. I used to enjoy those kinds of movies when I was a kid, with the bigger-than-life hero who stood up for the downtrodden or swashbuckled his way across the high seas." Tucker wiggled a little nearer, resting his head on Gerome's shoulder. "I never thought that I would end up in bed with one of them."

"Oh, come on," Gerome whispered. "That's not me, and you know it."

Tucker scoffed. "Really? You took in three homeless people and gave them a place to live and a chance at a new life. You helped me get a job, and you looked after me and Joshie. You even made it so that when Cheryl got sick, it was here with people who cared for her instead of in a camp somewhere. We have the chance to become a family, and I want that."

"Me too." That was what he wanted more than anything else. Having his old life back didn't even come close.

Tucker squeezed his hand and closed his eyes, and for the first time in his life, Gerome realized he had found the one thing he had always looked for and never thought he could have.

Epilogue

"YOU'RE HOME just in time," Gerome said as Tucker came in the door and set his books on the table. He was taking his first college classes with the hope of becoming a teacher someday. There were times when his life seemed to turn on a dime, and they had decided to use some of the money they'd "found" for his tuition. "How was it?"

"Awesome," he answered with a grin. Tucker was so excited he could burst.

And sometimes things happened a lot slower than anyone hoped. Cheryl's recovery took longer than anyone expected. They rented a larger place in the same complex so Joshie and Cheryl could each have their own room. Gerome took to a parenting role like a duck to water, giving Cheryl a chance to recover. Tucker was so damned proud of him.

No longer did Joshie have just a few toys. Tucker swore that as soon as they moved in, Gerome went on a shopping spree, outfitting Joshie's room with everything a little boy could want, including a bed shaped like a race car, matching curtains, and shelves anchored to the wall that were now packed with cars, Legos, and puzzles.

"What are we doing?" Joshie asked.

"We're going to have a party," Gerome answered. "On a boat."

Joshie jumped up and down, and Tucker wondered who was more excited, Joshie, or the really big boy Tucker was in love with.

"Why don't you get a few toys in a bag. This is a surprise for your mommy. Uncle Daniel took her to a spa to make her feel better, and he's going to bring her. So we need to hurry. Okay?"

Joshie raced away and came back with two trucks and a car. Tucker put them in the bag and added that to the things Gerome was taking out to the car. Tucker checked that everything was all set before helping Gerome get things loaded and Joshie settled in his car seat.

Tucker got in the car, and Gerome locked up before joining him, starting the car, and pulling out, taking his hand as he drove.

Sometimes Tucker found it hard to believe all the things he knew now about Gerome, though a lot of the time they felt like a story, detached from the man he knew and loved. The things Gerome had done were part of his past, but they didn't seem connected to the man he was now.

"You're holding hands," Joshie said from the back seat. "I wanna hold hands too."

"How about when we get to the boat? We can hold hands when we get on," Gerome offered, and Tucker thought he seemed happy. Who would have thought Gerome would be so parental.

"Are we there?" Joshie asked, bouncing in his seat. "I like boats."

Gerome rolled his eyes, and Tucker snickered. "Almost." He got impatient at times. Thankfully Gerome made the turn into the marina, and they all got out and made their way to the boat they had chartered for the evening. Gerome gave Joshie some things to carry, and they loaded themselves up.

Gerome got his stuff on the boat and then came back, taking Joshie's hand and making sure he got on and settled. "This is Captain Marty," Gerome explained.

"I understand this is a celebration?"

Joshie nodded. "We have chocolate cake." He had picked it out special.

"Is there anything I can do to help?" Marty asked as Richard, Coby, and Terrance arrived. "God, this is going to be one heck of a party." There was no doubt about it.

TUCKER HAD agreed to keep watch for Daniel and Cheryl. As soon as he saw their car, he hurried back to the boat, and everyone hid as best they could.

"Why are we here? I thought we were—"

As soon as they heard her voice, they all stood up and yelled, "Surprise!"

Joshie jumped up and down with excitement as Cheryl stepped onto the boat, and he hugged her tightly. "Were you really surprised?"

"I sure was," she said with a huge smile. The weeks of recovery from near kidney failure had been long and hard, with plenty of medication, diet regimens, and a lot of care. Joshie had been determined to help her, and with a lot of help and love, Cheryl had slowly returned from the brink, gaining strength every day.

"Are we ready to cast off?" Captain Marty asked.

"Aye-aye, Captain," Coby said, and Marty proceeded to remove the lines and maneuver the boat out of the marina and into the channel that led to the gulf.

Tucker sat on one of the benches on the starboard side with Gerome next to him. Daniel immediately began setting out the food. He really loved to feed people, and it was a party, after all.

"Did you think this was possible a few months ago?" Gerome asked.

"Nope." Tucker pulled a piece of paper from his pocket and handed it to Gerome. "I was so scared then, but I'm glad we never needed to use this."

Gerome looked it over and ripped it up into small pieces before placing it in the trash bag Daniel had brought along. He had a real, certified letter from Cheryl, along with wills and powers of attorney so that if anything were to happen to her, then Uncle Tucker and Uncle Gerome would raise Joshie.

"Things worked out in the end," Gerome said with a soft smile.

"Yeah, they did. But I don't want to have to go through all that again. Hopefully things will be better."

"Come on, guys. It's time to eat and party." Daniel turned on music and popped a bottle of champagne and one of sparkling grape juice for the boys and Cheryl. Then he filled glasses, and they raised them. "To Cheryl, for fighting so hard to come back to us."

Cheryl blushed but clinked plastic glasses with everyone, and then they drank.

"I wanna toast," Joshie said.

"Okay. What do you want to toast to?" Cheryl asked.

Joshie paused and then grinned. "To lots of new uncles." They raised their glasses once more.

"And to new nephews," Gerome added before they all sat down to a feast, with Tucker right beside Gerome, sharing a smile.

As the sun set on their pasts, Tucker knew a new day would dawn bright and full of possibilities. He leaned against Gerome and thought of their future… together… as a family.

Don't miss how the story began!

Bad to Be Good: Book One

Longboat Key, Florida, is about as far from the streets of Detroit as a group of gay former mobsters can get, but threats from within their own organization forced them into witness protection—and a new life.

Richard Marsden is making the best of his second chance, tending bar and learning who he is outside of organized crime… and flirting with the cute single dad, Daniel, who comes in every Wednesday. But much like Richard, Daniel hides dark secrets that could get him killed. When Daniel's past as a hacker catches up to him, Richard has the skills to help Daniel out, but not without raising some serious questions and risking his own new identity and the friends who went into hiding with him.

Solving problems like Daniel's is what Richard does best—and what he's trying to escape. But finding a way to keep Daniel and his son safe without sacrificing the person he's becoming will take some imagination, and the stakes have never been higher. This time it's not just lives on the line—it's his heart….

RICHARD MARSDEN—yes, that was his name now. It was always at the front of his mind that his old life was over. Everything had been stripped away, and the person and the life he'd had before were gone. And that included his real name. Well, now Marsden was his "real" name. At least it was supposed to be, but it didn't feel like it. Though to be fair, nothing about where he lived and what he did each day felt real to him. He doubted it ever would.

"I ain't never gonna get used to this shit," his brother Terrance grumped as he stalked into the empty bar, looking around. "You know what went down?" He came closer, stomping on the wooden floor. "A customer got in my face 'cause we didn't have the size flange that he needed, and I fucking had to stand there like a dope instead of ripping the fucker's head off."

Richard shot his hand out and smacked Terrance on the back of the head. "No talking about that stuff. Not here—or anywhere, for that matter. And no street talk. Remember that we need to speak *properly* so we don't stand out." He rolled his eyes and then puffed up his chest, glaring hard at his younger, but built like a brick shithouse, brother in spirit. "And no ripping anyone's head off," he added in a hiss just above a whisper. "Sometimes I wonder what the hell is wrong with you."

Terrance inhaled, and anger flared in his eyes but then abated slowly. "At least he isn't dead." That was better.

Richard took a deep breath, inhaling the scent of fish, ocean water, and whatever seasoning the guys in the kitchen were using. The damned stuff had been stoking his appetite since he arrived an hour ago. "What are you doing here instead of being at work?"

"Break. I walked down to cool off," Terrance said.

"Okay. Go on back to the hardware store and finish your shift, because you are not to get fired. And don't draw any extra attention to yourself. Remember the rules." He crooked his finger and lowered his voice. "If you do decide to rip anyone's head off, remember that yours is next. You know I'll do it, and piss down your damned neck. Now go back to work, and no talking about…. Just keep your mouth shut. You know how to do that."

Terrance nodded and turned away, leaving the bar and smacking the door shut with a bang. Richard picked up his tray of glasses, shaking his head as he went back to work stocking the bar for tonight.

It wasn't that Richard didn't understand how Terrance felt—he very much did. Richard had spent the past four months stocking glasses and getting drinks, listening to guys who sat at the bar bellyaching over the fact that they thought their wives were having an affair or that things at work were going to shit. Richard could tell them all about things going to hell. It had happened to them—him and his brothers—and now he was tending bar instead of running an entertainment organization. Now that was the shits of epic proportions.

Richard finished stocking and stepped outside the bar for a breath of fresh air. They didn't open for another half hour, and he was ready.

The sun beat down on the empty parking area, the Florida heat wafting off the blacktop. If he looked carefully across the street and between the houses and palm trees, he could see the Gulf of Mexico, the water sparkling as the waves caught the light. To most people, this would be paradise. Richard knew that, and yet he missed Detroit and his home. Yeah, to most people Detroit was not the kind of place you missed. Richard could understand that. But it was the city he'd grown up in, his home, and he had been somebody there. He thought he was going places, in line for big things, and then everything fucking changed at the drop of a hat, and just like that it was gone.

The familiar white Focus with the ding in the front bumper pulled into the parking area and up next to where he was standing. His youngest friend and brother from a different mother, Gerome, lowered the window. "I saw you standing out here. You out to get sunstroke or something?"

Richard rolled his eyes. "No. Getting some fresh, water-filled air before I go back inside and pretend to be a bartender." That was it—his entire life was pretend. "And we gotta have the 'keep your damn mouth shut' conversation with Terrance… again." He was getting so sick of this. For the millionth time he wondered if anything was ever going to be normal again. The answer that he kept coming back to was that it wasn't.

Richard, Terrance, and Gerome had been friends and a family of their own making since they were twelve years old. They'd survived on the mean streets of depressed inner-city Detroit by their wits and having each other's backs. The three of them joined the Garvic organization of the Italian mafia when they were fourteen and worked their way upward fast. They were tough as hell and none of them took any shit from anyone—or had to—because everyone in the organization knew that to take one of them on was to engage all three of them. They were tough, smart, and feared. Richard liked that.

In the end, the three of them had made a great deal of money for Harold Garvic. Richard ran the gay clubs in Detroit and was the king of the gay mafia… so to speak. He ran the entire enterprise and returned a great deal of money, managing the legitimate club façade while laundering millions in cash. Terrance was the muscle and feared well beyond their group. No one messed with any of them because no one in the Garvic organization wanted to see Terrance come through their door. Gerome was the idea man. He dreamed up new ways to make piles of money, and together the three of them made it happen. Life was fucking sweet.

Then Harold Sr. died, and his prick of a son didn't want to be involved in "their" kind of business. Instead of letting the three of them have their little piece of the empire, he made his first and biggest mistake: Harold Jr. came after them. Now the Garvic organization was a shadow of what it was, their leaders were doing decades behind bars, and Richard, Terrance, and Gerome had different lives, living on Longboat Key in Florida, abiding by a million rules so the government could keep them safe. They were three brothers in spirit who were now trying to figure things out in a world where they didn't understand the rules.

"All right, I'll talk to him." Gerome nodded, seeming resigned, his words pulling Richard out of his good-old-days fog. Of the three of them, Gerome had had the easiest time. He had been placed at a gift boutique that sold upscale tourist items. The thing was that Gerome could sell anything. He had rearranged the place within the first two weeks, asked about new items, and all of a sudden he was in charge of the sales floor when sales started going through the roof. At least one of them was doing okay. "I'll handle it. See you later." He raised the window and pulled out of the lot.

Richard took a deep breath, pushing away the hurt to his pride that each and every day seemed to bring, and went back inside. He had work to do. He checked that the kitchen was all right, then greeted Andi as she came in through the back door.

"Everything okay?" she asked.

Richard wiped the moroseness off his face, plastering on a professional mask. "Sure. You all set?" He went behind the bar to cut limes and lemons for garnish, taking a second as she wound through the floor of tables that looked as though they had been through one of Florida's tropical storms and come out the other side. The chairs had seen the wear from hundreds of butts, and the walls, darkened with age and constant exposure to humid salt air, were decorated with mounted fish and old buoys, as well as pictures of great catches. The entire place seemed to have soaked up the scent of the sea, fish, and water.

"You know me. I'm always ready." She gave him a little swing of her hips and then turned away. Andi was one of the few people outside of the guys who knew that he was gay. She had made a play for him the first week he'd worked at the bar, and he had turned her down. To tell the truth, she was attractive, with shoulder-length black hair, a great figure, and intense eyes.

"Too bad you never go for a guy who would deserve you," he muttered and returned to work as the first patrons came through the front door.

The bar patrons were a combination of tourists and locals. A few of the people he saw all the time came in and took familiar places at the bar. Richard pulled beers and made drinks, started tabs, and took payment, the cash settling in his hand before going to the register.

That had been one of the hardest things to remember. In Detroit it was expected that he would skim a certain amount off the top. Richard and Gerome were masters of it, and he'd always been conscientious about returning a growing amount to Harold, which had kept him happy.

"Happy Wednesday," Tim, one of the regulars, said, and Richard's mind skipped a track for a second. He had completely forgotten, and now some of the gloom lifted from inside him.

Richard filled an order from Andi and continued his tasks with half an eye on the front door as he worked.

He knew when it was six o'clock because Daniel came into the bar.

Richard had no idea what it was about this slim man with intense brown eyes and surfer-length black hair hanging to just below his ears that drew him, but as long as Daniel was in the bar, Richard knew exactly where he was at all times, even when his back was turned.

Daniel took a place at the bar.

"You want your usual?" He was already pulling Daniel's beer without really thinking about it. Once Daniel nodded, he placed the beer on the scarred bar surface in front of him.

"The fish and chips, please," Daniel said in his soft voice. Then he flashed him a smile. Richard was determined not to allow his heart rate to rise, but the fucking thing did it anyway. He leaned over the bar just a little, almost as though Daniel had a gravity of his own and Richard was caught in it.

"Of course. I'll put your order in right away," Richard said and swallowed hard, licking his lips as their gazes locked for the fraction of a second. Then Richard remembered where they were and that this was not a gay club in Detroit, but the Cormorant on Longboat Key, Florida.

"Thank you," Daniel said without turning away. "I really appreciate that."

Richard had to break whatever was going on between them. Not that he wasn't excited, but damn, if he wasn't careful, someone was going to come in, and if they joined him behind the bar, there was no damned way they could miss how much Daniel got under his skin.

"Can I get another beer?" Mike asked from a few seats down.

Richard pulled himself away, poured the beer, and put in Daniel's order through the system. At least he could breathe for a few seconds.

Not that this attraction and the innocent flirting he did with Daniel on occasion were ever going to lead anywhere. They couldn't, not in a million years. It didn't matter how many times Richard wondered just what that lithe, compact body looked like under those worn jeans that hugged him like a second skin or the dark blue polo shirt with the tiny hole right at the collar where it sometimes rubbed at Daniel's neck.

Richard, Terrance, and Gerome were only here and stayed alive because they were doing their best to abide by the rules of the Witness Protection Program, and that meant they all needed to stay out of the public eye, not draw attention to themselves, and definitely not tell anyone anything about their past. But more than that, they had had to plead to be allowed to stay together. If they messed up, they wouldn't just be relocated, but separated as well. Sure, Richard could have a fling with Daniel and then they could go on their separate ways, but Richard knew that if he got a single taste of him, he'd want more. Daniel was like potato chips. One would never be enough.

He checked on Daniel's order with the kitchen and refilled glasses, telling himself he was going to ignore Daniel and do his job, keeping himself busy until he left. Daniel had a routine almost as regular as clockwork. Each Wednesday he came in a few minutes after six, had a beer, ordered fish and chips, and nursed his second beer until just before nine o'clock, when he said good night and left the bar. It had been that way since Richard's first week on the job. Richard had tried to talk with him on occasion, and other than his name and a little small talk, he'd learned nothing about him. Richard had cracked some of the hardest men, actually reducing them to tears when he was in charge of the clubs. But hell, Daniel could give lessons on keeping your mouth shut.

When Daniel's order was ready, Richard went to the kitchen to get it, returned, and placed it in front of him. Daniel reached for his cutlery and his hand brushed against Richard's. The gesture was completely innocent and accidental, and yet Richard nearly gasped at the shock that raced through him all the way to his bones.

"Thank you," Daniel said.

Richard nodded and turned away to go back to work, frustration building high enough that he felt it in his temples like the start of a headache, except this held a touch of the delicious and the forbidden, which only made him want it all the more, even though he told himself repeatedly that Daniel—or anyone at all—was off-limits.

ANDREW GREY is the author of more than one hundred works of Contemporary Gay Romantic fiction. After twenty-seven years in corporate America, he has now settled down in Central Pennsylvania with his husband, Dominic, and his laptop. An interesting ménage. Andrew grew up in western Michigan with a father who loved to tell stories and a mother who loved to read them. Since then he has lived throughout the country and traveled throughout the world. He is a recipient of the RWA Centennial Award, has a master's degree from the University of Wisconsin–Milwaukee, and now writes full-time. Andrew's hobbies include collecting antiques, gardening, and leaving his dirty dishes anywhere but in the sink (particularly when writing). He considers himself blessed with an accepting family, fantastic friends, and the world's most supportive and loving partner. Andrew currently lives in beautiful, historic Carlisle, Pennsylvania.

Email: andrewgrey@comcast.net
Website: www.andrewgreybooks.com